You Are Not My Son

First Edition, 2016

ISBN: 978-1537129983

Jay Argent
jay@jayargent.com

www.jayargent.com

You Are Not My Son

Jay Argent

Prologue

18 YEARS AGO

A broad smile on his face, Paul Wesley entered Frank's Garden and saw some of his workmates already sitting around a large table at the end of the bar. They were celebrating his promotion, which meant that the men were now his subordinates. That gave him a lot of satisfaction, but he did his best not to let it show.

"Hi, Paul! We've been waiting for you," Thomas Hanson shouted, "and congratulations!"

"Thanks, Tommy," Paul replied cheerfully.

Five years ago, both Thomas and Paul had started at Henderson Watson Sport, which was a rapidly growing retailer of sports clothes and equipment. The firm had opened a big shop at Fairmont, and the friends from college had applied for jobs there.

"Or is it now 'Mr. Wesley' for us?" Thomas joked, and the group laughed at the comment.

"Shut up," Paul said but couldn't help enjoying the attention.

"Maybe we should call you 'The Greatest,'" one of the men said. At Paul's confused frown, the man explained, "You know, like Muhammad Ali, the famous boxer."

Thomas looked at Paul, who went silent for a while. He knew that Paul had been a boxer in high school but had been forced to quit. Paul had never wanted to share the whole story, but rumor had it that he had had difficulties keeping his fists away from fights outside the ropes.

"I think 'Paul' will work," he said and gestured for the waiter to bring him a glass of beer.

A couple more colleagues soon joined them, and the group spent a nice Friday evening together drinking beer and talking about everything and nothing. When last call was announced, most of them had already left for home. Only Paul and Thomas were standing near the counter.

"I think you really deserved it," Thomas said. "The promotion, I mean."

"Yeah," Paul replied. He was drunk and searching for words. "At least, we need the extra money. Sara's been at home taking care of the baby," he said finally.

"Man, I envy you. You got a beautiful wife and now this kid."

"If that god damn brat would just let me sleep at night," Paul said, but regretted the comment. Becoming a father had been one of the highlights of his life.

"They say kids grow old sooner than you realize," Thomas said.

They were the last customers at the bar, and the bartender was giving them looks to get them to leave, too. Apparently, the man wanted to close the place and head for home. Paul and Thomas took the hint, and they were soon walking to the parking area.

"You're so not driving," Thomas said as he opened the front door of his car to Paul.

"Thanks for ... driving me home," Paul slurred as he climbed into the front seat of his friend's car without objection.

"Of course, boss," Thomas joked and started the engine.

It didn't take long for Thomas to drive to the house where Paul and Sara Wesley lived, and it wasn't the first time he had escorted Paul home after spending hours at a bar. He helped Paul out of the car and watched as his friend staggered toward the front door. Finally, Paul found the key in his pocket and got the door open.

"Where have you been?" Sara Wesley asked as soon as her husband stepped in. Her eyes looked tired, and her hair was scruffy, but above all, her tone was full of anger.

"I was ... I was at the bar," Paul said as matter-of-factly as he could after far too many glasses of beer. He didn't need his wife's permission to have fun with his friends.

"You think it's fair that you spent all night drinking, and I'm here alone changing Alex's diapers?" Sara said.

"You're the woman in this house. A man's gotta do what a man's gotta do," Paul said.

If he'd thought that Sara would appreciate his drunken humor at this time of the night, he couldn't have been more mistaken. Pissed off, Sara stomped to the nearby table and snatched up the only boxing trophy Paul had ever won. She slammed it to the floor, sending shards flying all over the living room.

"Fucking bitch!" Paul yelled and stepped closer to his wife.

"You were a lousy boxer, but you're an even worse father!" Sara yelled back.

Alex started to cry in the bedroom, but Paul didn't care. Without thinking, he punched Sara, his fist colliding with her left cheekbone just below her eye. Sara fell on the floor, hurting her left arm.

"Shit. I'm … sorry. Honey, I'm so sorry," Paul murmured as soon as he realized what he had done.

"Leave," Sara said and glared at her husband. "Now," she added.

She didn't have to ask twice.

A week later, Paul and Sara were sitting on the couch in their living room. Paul had baby Alex on his lap. Alex was smiling at him and tried to take hold of his fingers with his small hands. Sara didn't smile, and she didn't make an attempt to touch her husband, either.

"Thanks for letting me come back," Paul said, looking at the opposite wall. "Tommy's sofa isn't very comfortable," he added, trying to lighten the atmosphere.

"I don't want Alex to grow up without a father," Sara said.

"Me neither," Paul said quickly.

"But I still don't know what I think about you and all this."

"I see."

Paul's voice was quiet, and Sara heard regret in his tone for the first time. Maybe Paul was sincerely sorry for hitting her. He had always had somewhat rustic manners, and he talked only when he had something to say and never about his feelings. And that was exactly what made him a real man in Sara's eyes. That was why she had fallen in love with Paul.

"I booked you a therapy session on Monday," Sara said.

"What? Therapy?" Paul said, and was about to object but closed his mouth. Apparently, this was something nonnegotiable.

"It's anger management therapy," she said. "It's my condition for you coming back home."

"Okay," Paul said, trying to hide his annoyance.

"I'll go start dinner," Sara said as she left for the kitchen.

Six-month-old Alex babbled happily on Paul's lap. He smiled at the boy and couldn't help feeling proud. Paul hadn't told Sara, but when she got pregnant, his biggest dream had been that the baby would be a boy. And now he was holding his firstborn on his lap.

"One day, you're gonna be a great athlete," Paul said to Alex. "You'll be a tough man like your daddy."

Alex stopped babbling and looked at his father like he had understood. Paul found it funny and stroked Alex's thin blond hair. When the boy was older, he would take him to play baseball or football, and he would be there in the front row to cheer him on.

"And then you'll find a beautiful girl. As beautiful as your mother," Paul said, speaking both to Alex and himself. "My boy," he added and rocked the baby.

Sara was listening in the kitchen. It was the first time she had heard Paul talking to Alex like that. Maybe it was a good sign, and she agreed that their sweet baby would become a handsome man who would someday melt someone's heart.

Little did they know that that someone would be another boy, and eighteen years later their baby would be moving into a shared dorm room with him. Technically speaking, they didn't know it when it happened.

Chapter 1

TODAY

"This is the last one," Liam said, carrying a box filled with his laptop and some books. He found an empty spot on the floor and carefully set the box down.

"Good. I'll go park the car," Alex said and ran down the stairs to the lobby.

Liam could hardly believe it. He and Alex were now freshmen at Eastwood University, and they were even sharing a dorm room on campus. The room wasn't big, but for Liam, the only thing that mattered was that he and Alex were together. *If this is a dream, please don't wake me up*, Liam thought.

Soon, Alex came back and wiped sweat from his forehead. Liam's laughter died on his lips as took in the way Alex's soaked t-shirt was glued to his athletic body.

It highlighted his muscular chest and made the blond-haired swimmer look shockingly sexy. There were clear advantages to choosing a hot day to move into an old dorm that didn't have air conditioning.

"I need a shower," Alex said as he took his shirt off and started to search for the bag where he had his towel.

"Yes, you do," Liam said, unable to take his eyes off his hot boyfriend. "I'll put the groceries in the fridge and make us a snack," he added.

The shower room was at the end of the hall. It was one big space without curtains or screens, and the spigots were along the wall on both sides of the room. Memories of the high school swim team filled Alex's mind as soon as he entered the empty room. While he and Liam had heard some noise from the third floor as they were carrying in boxes, it seemed that most of the students had not arrived on campus yet.

Alex took the shower closest to the door and let the water rinse the sweat from his body before washing with the handmade cocoa vanilla soap. It had been a gift from Liam, who loved its smell. Feeling a familiar tingle in his crotch, Alex forced himself to stop thinking of Liam sniffing his naked body.

With the towel wrapped around his waist, Alex returned to the room and found Liam waiting there with two soda pops and pizza slices, which he had heated in the microwave.

"Cool. My boyfriend is a top chef," Alex joked.

"Shut up," Liam said as he wrapped his arms around Alex.

While they hugged and kissed, Liam pulled away Alex's towel and let it drop on the floor. He caressed Alex's bare butt and pulled his boyfriend, who was five inches taller than him, close against his body. Alex purred softly and stroked the hair at the nape of Liam's neck.

"I love you," Alex whispered in Liam's ear.

"I love you, too," Liam said and kissed Alex. "Let's eat before this gourmet dinner gets cold," he added, taking Alex's towel.

"Hey," Alex protested, "can I get that back?"

"No. I like the way you look," Liam said and passed Alex his drink.

Feeling Liam's gaze on his crotch, Alex sat down on the bed and began to eat his pizza. He hadn't realized how hungry he was until he took his first bite. Pepperoni, pineapple, and hot, melted cheese were delicious—and his favorite. Alex smiled at Liam, who had chosen the toppings. Apparently, his cute boyfriend knew what he liked.

"Our first meal here," Liam said, turning to look at Alex with his beautiful brown eyes.

"Your parents were pretty excited that we got this room," Alex said.

"They really like you," Liam said. "Well, not as much as I do," he added and grinned.

"I wish I could say the same about my parents," Alex said, his face growing serious.

As Alex had packed the car that morning, his mother had been there to wish him a safe trip to Eddington. His father had been sitting inside reading the newspaper, saying hardly a word the entire morning. All of them had known that Alex was on his way to Liam's house, and that they would be sharing a dorm room. None of them had mentioned it, though. Alex had been avoiding the topic as much as his parents had.

"Do your parents suspect we're dating?" Liam asked, as if he could read Alex's mind. His boyfriend had been a bit quiet the whole day, and Liam was worried that something had happened in the morning.

"No," Alex said quickly. "If they did, they would stop paying my tuition."

"I still can't understand why Rick, or someone else, didn't tell your parents that we danced together at the prom," Liam said.

"Please, don't remind me about that douchebag." Alex snorted.

Rick Donovan, who used to be Alex's best friend, had blackmailed Alex throughout their senior year in high school and got him to date a girl in their class, which had almost ruined his relationship with Liam.

"I don't get it. How could you forgive me for that thing with Sarah?" Alex said, still feeling embarrassed.

Liam gave Alex an empathic look. "Oh, my sexy jock, haven't we talked about that a million times already? Can we just forget it?" he said. To assure his boyfriend that he meant it, he stood from his seat and moved to sit on Alex's lap.

Alex, who was still naked on the bed, wrapped his arms tightly around his small and skinny boyfriend. Liam was amazing, so kind and cute. Even though Alex couldn't tell his parents about them, he had decided

16

that they would be out on campus. He owed that to Liam. Besides, hiding their relationship had almost ruined it once, and Alex had no intention of going through that again.

Liam was just about to tell Alex how much he loved him when his phone started to ring. He pulled it from his pocket and noticed that his mother was calling. He decided to answer where he was, sitting there cozy on Alex's lap.

"Hi, Mom," Liam said and pushed his hair away from his face. He had let his dark hair grow out over the summer, and now it was constantly blocking his view.

"Hi, honey. How are you? Are you and Alex already on campus?" Jenny Green said avidly when she heard her son's voice on the other end of the line.

"Yeah, we are here," Liam said.

"Tell me everything. How was your trip there?"

Amused by his mother's enthusiasm, Liam started to describe their journey from Fairmont to Eddington. Just as he was explaining how big a city Eddington was, he felt Alex unbuckling his belt. Next, his jeans were unzipped, and Alex's hand found his penis and pulled it through the fly of his boxers.

"Did you remember to give Alex money for gas?" Jenny asked.

"Um … yes, of course," Liam said. He looked down and saw Alex rubbing his rapidly growing erection. Liam spread his legs, encouraging Alex to continue.

"Tell me about school. Have you met other students yet?" she asked.

"No, we just arrived," Liam said, trying to focus on the call.

Alex's hand felt great even though it made it hard for Liam to concentrate on the phone call. The whole six-hour trip to Eddington, he had waited for the opportunity to fool around with Alex. The way Alex was teasing him made him horny—a bit too horny, as a matter of fact.

"Yeah, Eddington is a … a nice city," Liam said to his mother as he tried to stop Alex stroking his erection.

To Liam's surprise, Alex used his left hand to capture Liam's arm and continued playing with Liam's penis with his other hand. Liam tried to stand up, but the strong jock was able to hold him in place on his lap. He stopped fighting and gave in to his boyfriend.

"How about the room? What's it like?" Liam's mother asked.

"Um … it's … nice," Liam said, trying to breathe normally.

"I'm not gonna stop," Alex whispered alluringly in his ear.

Liam was mortified. Even though he enjoyed what Alex was doing, shooting his load while talking with his mother would be beyond embarrassing. But no matter how hard he tried, he could not hold back much longer, and his mother didn't show any sign of ending the call anytime soon.

"You guys must be starving. Have you eaten anything?" she asked.

"Yes … I did some…," Liam began to say when he lost control. He tried to hold his breath as he came in multiple spurts all over his green t-shirt and black jeans.

"Oh, you're such a naughty boy," Alex whispered.

"Liam, are you still there?" his mother asked.

"Yeah, sorry. I'm still here," Liam said, hoping that his mother couldn't hear that he was panting. "Just got … interrupted," he added, and a broad smile appeared on his face. It had felt fantastic despite the totally improper timing.

I'm definitely going to make him pay for that, Liam thought when Alex passed him a box of tissues to clean his clothes. He was still holding the phone with his other hand and listening to his mother ramble on about how she and his father had been cleaning the house all day after the boys had left in the morning.

Alex blew him a kiss, and somehow Liam was sure that Alex would keep reminding him about this the rest of their time at Eastwood. Still, he could feel nothing but love toward his hot boyfriend. Alex was his swimmer boy, and they were meant to be together. Liam was sure about that.

The following morning, Liam woke up to someone kissing him. It didn't take long for him to realize that it was Alex and that it was their first morning in their new home. They had pushed the twin beds together the previous night so that they could sleep together.

"Morning, sunshine," Alex said, smiling broadly. Liam laughed at his bedhead but kissed him back.

"I'm starving," Liam said.

"And horny," Alex said as he pushed his hand under Liam's blanket.

"Mmm … maybe breakfast can wait a bit," Liam admitted, looking into Alex's big blue eyes.

An hour later, they had taken a short shower and were dressed for breakfast. They had some cereal in their small kitchen, but both of them wanted to walk around campus and find a cafeteria.

Liam checked his phone and found there was a message from his mother wishing them a happy first day at college. He felt it was a bit premature as classes wouldn't start until the following Monday.

"I'm a little jealous," Alex said after they had walked out of the front door of the dorm. "Your parents are so cool about us."

"You really think your parents would disown you if you told them about us?" Liam asked.

For the past two weeks, Alex had been pondering whether to tell his parents that he was gay. He felt bad leaving without them knowing the truth about their son, but he just couldn't do it. His parents wouldn't understand, and he needed their financial support.

"I know you expected the worst, and then your parents were so cool about you … being gay," Alex said.

"Yes, they were."

"I just wish mine would be, too, but I just … I know they wouldn't be."

Even though Liam wanted badly to disagree, he knew that Alex was right. He had seen Alex's parents only a couple of times over the summer, and those encounters had been awkward. Both of them knew that Liam was gay. Alex's mother tried to be polite, but Liam could sense that she wasn't pleased that Alex was spending time with him. Mr. Wesley, on the other hand, did his best to avoid him completely.

"It's funny. We live together now," Liam said, changing the topic to something lighter.

"Yes, we do," Alex said, flashing a smile at Liam. "Roommate," he added.

"Huh, I thought I was more to you," Liam said, pretending to be hurt.

"Yes, you are. A sexy boytoy," Alex laughed and poked Liam's arm.

Liam was happy that Alex was in a better mood. He had been quiet as they drove from Fairmont to Eastwood. Even though he had claimed that everything was fine, Liam knew that something had been bothering Alex. He knew his boyfriend, and he was pretty sure it had something to do with Alex's parents.

"Hi there!" someone shouted. Liam and Alex turned and saw two students coming from the dorm next to theirs.

"I'm Tyler, and this is my roommate," the more talkative of them said, pointing to the tall, muscular guy standing next to him.

"I'm Scott," he offered.

"I'm Alex, and this is Liam," Alex introduced them. "We just got here yesterday. We're looking for somewhere to get some breakfast."

"So, you're freshmen, too," Tyler said.

Alex nodded and scanned the guys. They had to be jocks; at least, both of them had rather athletic bodies. Tyler especially was easy on the eyes. He was slim and a bit taller than Alex, but had blond hair and blue eyes just like him. Alex tried to be cautious and not stare too long.

"I'm from Loveland, Colorado," said Tyler. "Don't laugh; there is such a city north of Denver." Tyler gave a winning smile and added, "That dumb jock is from Texas," as he motioned to Scott.

"Look who's talking," Scott said. "Loveland swimmer."

"So, where are you guys from?" Tyler asked.

"We're from Fairmont," Alex said.

"Both of you? So you know each other from high school?" Tyler said.

"Yeah, we were friends in high school. We're sharing a dorm room," Alex said, pointing to the building behind them.

"Oh, that's cool," Tyler said.

High school friends. How cool is that? Liam thought and looked at Alex, who got the message. The night of their high school prom, Alex had promised Liam that, as soon as they had moved to Eddington, they wouldn't have to keep their relationship hidden. Old habits die hard.

The four of them continued walking toward the Eastwood University main building. Alex mentioned to Tyler that he was on the high school swim team, too, which led to Tyler explaining all his swimming accomplishments ever since he was born. The others hardly had a chance to say anything. Soon they found a quiet fast food place and decided to stop to eat there.

"So, are you a swimmer, too?" Tyler asked Liam after they sat down at a table.

"No," Liam said, feeling a bit shy. He was hardly muscular enough to be an athlete. "I'm not good at any sports."

"What are you good at then?" Tyler asked, studying Liam.

"Um … I play the piano," Liam said with a blush and pushed a strand of hair away from his face.

"Cool," Tyler said. "My sister plays the violin. I can't play anything, and I'm the worst singer on the planet."

Scott cut in, talking about how he was a high school football player from Austin and was here because he got a scholarship to play for Eastwood. Scott's story reminded Alex of his failure to earn an athletic scholarship and how his parents were now paying his tuition.

"I wish I had been chosen for the swim team, too," Alex said, feeling a bit jealous of Tyler and Scott, who had been recruited for the university's teams.

"Yeah, it sucks that the team is so small," Tyler said, trying to comfort Alex. "But hey, why don't you join the swim club? They even organize national championships against other club swimming teams," he proposed.

It wasn't a bad idea, and Alex got a bit excited. "Yeah, why not?" he said, his good mood returning. Even though he wouldn't become a professional, his body longed for some exercise.

"Besides, you have more time for studies and girls if you don't have practice every day," Tyler said and smirked.

Alex forced a smile and pondered whether he should tell the jocks that he wasn't interested in girls. Despite his promise to Liam to be open about their relationship, he felt that something was holding him back. Regardless, before he could open his mouth, Tyler had already switched topics.

"By any chance, do you guys happen to have a car?" Tyler asked.

"I do," Alex said. "Why?"

"We were planning to visit the mall a couple of miles from here," Tyler said.

"Of course, we can take the bus, so that you don't—" Scott began to speak.

"It's not a problem. Let's go there together," Alex said, pleased that they had made some new friend so quickly. Tyler and Scott seemed like cool guys.

"Is that okay with you?" Alex asked Liam.

"Sure. That sounds like fun," Liam said, equally excited.

They walked back to the dorm where Alex and Liam had their room. Scott and Tyler followed them to the second floor and waited as Alex got his key to open the door. Only after they had stepped in did Alex realize that their beds were still joined together.

"This room looks just like ours in the other building," Tyler said. Then he paused. "Are you guys sleeping together?"

Alex blushed and didn't know what to say.

Chapter 2

Paul Wesley ran along the corridor to the meeting room. He was already late, and it didn't help that the arrogant young police officer had given him a speeding ticket on the highway from Fairmont to Buonas. Panting, he knocked on the door and stepped into the bright room.

"Morning, Paul," Stephen Brownlee said and checked his watch. The gray-haired old man in an expensive, custom-tailored suit and patent leather shoes was the Senior Director for North American Retail at Henderson Watson Sport.

"Good Morning, Mr. Brownlee," Paul said as he took a seat. "I apologize for being late."

The Senior Director glanced at his subordinate, who tried to calm down his breathing. Paul was wearing jeans, and his casual jacket covered most of the yellow dress shirt that should have been washed some days ago.

"I still have fifteen minutes, so let's get directly to business," Mr. Brownlee said. "How are things in Fairmont?"

Paul wiped sweat from his bald head and started to explain how they had recently renovated the office. He also mentioned the annual summer party that he had organized for his staff. He had worked for the firm over twenty years, and he had known most of his employees for a long time. They were almost like a family.

Mr. Brownlee browsed his phone while Paul was speaking, and only after Paul had finished did he put the phone away and raise his gaze to Paul.

"Paul, your sales numbers are a big concern for me," Mr. Brownlee said.

For God's sake, it's the fucking economic crisis. Nobody buys anything these days, Paul thought but kept his poker-face. He knew that Mr. Brownlee wasn't interested in hearing any excuses.

"Yes, sir. I agree that we could do better," Paul said evenly, rubbing his hands across his big belly.

"I don't need your agreement," Mr. Brownlee said. "I need actions from you."

"I can start planning a marketing campaign," Paul offered.

"How you do it isn't my concern. I'm asking you to increase your sales by twenty percent during the next quarter, and I don't want to see a drop in the margin," Mr. Brownlee said. "Can you deliver that for me?"

"Yes, sir," Paul said, even though he had no idea how that was possible.

Paul had taken over the leadership of the Fairmont retail shop three years ago after the previous store manager had retired. He had to admit that the business hadn't been growing under his leadership.

"Any other business?" Mr. Brownlee asked and stood up before Paul had time to answer.

"No, sir," Paul said.

"Okay, then, see you later," Mr. Brownlee said as he walked to the door. "And Paul, please take this seriously. I don't want to start looking for a new store manager," he added before leaving the room.

Paul walked by the window and hit the frame so hard that, for a short moment, he was afraid that the window would break. The expectations that Mr. Brownlee was setting for him were unrealistic—and he knew that he would likely lose his job if he didn't meet them.

Once he had calmed down, he marched along the corridor back to the elevators. He didn't even look at the friendly young lady at the reception desk when we walked out of the Henderson Watson Sport local headquarters. He had to figure out something to save his job.

Sara was cooking dinner when Paul returned from work. After the meeting with the senior executive, he had driven back to Fairmont and spent the rest of the day in his office going through all the financial reports from the past few months. The more he read, the more frustrated he became.

"Hi, honey. How was your day?" Sara greeted him when he entered the kitchen.

"It was okay," Paul said.

"You met your boss this morning. Did he promise you that raise?" she asked.

"Hmm … let's see how it goes," he said.

Sara took the casserole from the oven and set the table. Since Alex was no longer at home, it was just the two of them eating dinner. Even though both Paul and Sara spent a lot of time at work, suddenly the house seemed empty. Their only child had become a man and left the nest.

"I wonder how Alex is doing. He didn't call yesterday, but they should be settled in by now," Sara said.

"I still can't understand why he chose to live with that … that gay kid." Paul snorted.

"Something happened at the prom, and Alex broke up with that girl," Sara said. "I didn't want to push him. He was so sad and wanted to share a room with his friend."

"Fine. As long as that kid doesn't turn my son gay," he said and continued eating.

Taking a deep breath, Sara looked at her husband. At Eastwood, all freshmen were expected to live on campus. If Alex had to live with someone, Liam at least took his studies seriously. For the next academic year, she could rent Alex an off-campus residence. She hoped Liam wouldn't tell anyone about his choice of lifestyle so that it would not label her son while they were still sharing a room.

"It's six-hour drive there. Maybe we could visit Alex some weekend?" Sara said.

"I'm quite busy at work right now," Paul said.

"Honey, just one weekend. I miss him already."

"Fine. But not this weekend. Sometime later."

After dinner, Paul left his wife to clean the kitchen. He went to his office and closed the door behind him. Then he opened his laptop and started to make calculations. By midnight, Paul had come to a conclusion that one of the biggest problems his store had was their sales to local sports clubs.

After he became the store manager, Paul had chosen Alma Hanson to manage their cooperation with the local sports clubs. It had been a mistake, which he had known even when he made the appointment. He had promoted Alma because she was married to his college friend, Thomas, who had left the firm a long time ago and was nowadays coaching the swim team at Fairmont High School. In fact, Coach Hanson had been coaching Alex.

Without Tommy, I wouldn't have my family, Paul thought, remembering the time when Alex had been a baby and he had been spending most of his time at bars drinking beer with his friends. It had been Thomas who had offered his sofa when Sara kicked him out of their home. Paul had gone through anger management therapy, but he still felt that Thomas had talked more sense into him than the therapist.

The financial reports were depressing. To get more money for marketing and other activities to lure more customers, Paul had to lay off some of his employees. Ironically enough, at the summer party just a few weeks ago, he had vowed he would take good care of his employees.

Sara opened the door and interrupted him. "Honey, are you still working?" she asked.

"Huh, what time is it?" Paul said, glancing at the clock on the wall. "This was so exciting that I didn't realize how late it was," he added and closed his laptop.

"Your boss must be happy that you are working so hard," she said.

"I hope so," Paul said, avoiding eye contact with his wife as they went to bed.

On Sunday evening, Paul and Sara were having dinner at a restaurant. While they were waiting for their appetizers, Sara kept complaining about one demanding client she had to meet the following day. Paul stayed quiet and sipped his beer with such speed that his glass was almost empty when the waiter brought their food.

"Could you please bring me another?" Paul said, pointing to the glass. The waiter nodded and left.

"Is everything okay?" Sara asked. "You look tired."

"All fine. You have nothing to worry about," Paul assured her.

He looked at his wife, who wore a beautiful dress, and wondered why it was so difficult for him to tell her about the discussion with Mr. Brownlee. She would find out anyway if he were fired. Maybe it was his pride that prevented him from opening up about his problems.

"I called Alex this morning," Sara said.

"How was he?" Paul asked.

"He was in his room preparing for his first day at college."

"Has he made any friends yet?"

"He said he met two other freshmen. I can't remember their names, but one is a swimmer, and the other is a football player."

Paul was happy to hear that Alex was making friends with other athletes. His son would have normal guys with whom to study and exercise, especially if Alex's roommate began to hang around with his kind of people.

"Is it a bit hot in here?" Sara asked.

"Why? I don't think so," Paul said, surprised.

"Maybe it was just some spice in the food," she said and drank water from her glass. "I think I'll visit the ladies room," she added and stood up.

Paul watched as his wife walked through the restaurant to the restroom. Then he turned to look at his starter plate that the waiter hadn't yet collected. He studied the leftovers but could not understand what could have been so spicy in the breaded mushrooms.

"Is everything okay here?" the waiter asked as he took Sara's plate.

"Sure," Paul said. "It was delicious."

"Thank you, sir," the waiter said. "Your main course will be ready soon." With that, he left with the plates.

A couple of minutes later, Sara came back. She looked a bit pale, but she reassured her husband that she felt fine. Paul nodded and told her that they would get more to eat soon.

"I wonder why there are so many people on Sunday," Paul said and looked around.

Sara didn't reply. She lifted her water glass and drank it empty. Paul poured her more from the jug that the waiter had brought.

"Are you sure you're okay?" Paul asked.

There was still no reply from Sara, but Paul saw that her eyes were glassy. Then her head began to sway from side to side. Paul realized that something was wrong, and he barely managed to stand up and catch his wife before she fainted.

"Somebody, call an ambulance!" he shouted and tried to wake her up.

She didn't wake, and the minutes stretched until Paul finally heard the sound of the sirens when the paramedics arrived.

Chapter 3

Alex sat in a big auditorium and listened carefully to the math professor. It was the Friday of his first week at college, and he was pretty excited about everything. All the teachers seemed cool, and the atmosphere on campus was relaxed. Besides, he would be seeing his cute boyfriend soon.

Liam's big dream had been fulfilled when he was accepted to the history program. Alex's original plan had been to study law like his mother, but after some consideration, Alex had chosen computer engineering, which meant that they shared hardly any classes. It didn't matter since they lived in the same room and could see each other every evening, and every night.

As soon as the lecture finished, Alex hurried to the park that was behind the main building. A lot of students were there already, lying on the grass and enjoying the sunny afternoon. A bit farther, in the shadow of a maple tree, Alex saw Liam waiting for him. He was wearing a red hoodie, which fit perfectly with his black hair and made him look especially cute to Alex.

"Mom called me just before math," Alex said as he plopped down beside his boyfriend.

"Did something happen?" Liam asked, noticing that Alex sounded a bit anxious.

"She fainted in a restaurant."

"Where? When?"

"On Sunday. They took her to the hospital and ran some tests but found nothing."

"So, she's okay now?"

"Yeah. Maybe she was just stressed or something."

Liam found it strange that Alex's mom had called only now, almost a week later. If his mother had been taken to a hospital, his parents would inform him right away. He debated bringing that up to Alex but decided to leave it alone.

Changing the subject, Liam said, "Tyler's on his way home for the weekend, but I invited Scott to eat with us," Liam said. "I hope you don't mind?"

"Of course not," Alex said.

"You remember when they realized that we're a couple? You were as red as a fire truck," Liam teased his boyfriend.

"Ha-ha," Alex said, blushing again slightly.

After seeing their beds together, it hadn't taken long for Tyler to realize that Alex and Liam were more than friends. He had been totally cool about it, and it didn't seem to bother Scott either. At least, they had all continued on their way to the mall, where they'd had a good time. And now, Scott would be meeting them so they could all have dinner together.

"I'm actually relieved that I don't have to live with my parents anymore," Alex said. "Does that make me a bad person?" He glanced at Liam's brown eyes.

"I don't think so," Liam said before a long pause. "But we can't keep this secret from them forever. One day, they will learn about us."

"I know," Alex said. "I know."

Out of the blue, Alex kissed Liam, who rested his hand on Alex's thigh and kissed him back. They were in the park surrounded by students, two college boys kissing each other, and nobody paid any attention.

"Wow. That was … unexpected," Liam said. "But nice," he added, beaming.

"I've realized something," Alex said, and his face got serious. "I've been so afraid of what my parents would think of me that I almost let it ruin our relationship."

"Alex, it's okay. I understand," Liam said.

"No, it's not okay," Alex said and kissed Liam again.

"So, you don't mind if all these people see us kissing?" Liam asked.

"No, but what I do mind a bit is that your hand is giving me a freaking boner."

"What makes you think I'm not doing it on purpose?"

Alex pushed Liam's hand away and adjusted his crotch. Then he kissed Liam one more time. He would be lying if he claimed that the public display of affection didn't make him a bit uncomfortable. Still, being able to kiss Liam like all other couples did in the park filled his heart with such an overwhelming happiness that it defeated all his fears.

"Hey, guys. What's up?" Scott said. Neither Alex nor Liam had seen him coming as they were too focused on each other.

"More than you think," Liam said, and grinned at Alex.

"Eh…," Scott frowned, unsure what Liam meant, "are you hungry?"

"Sure, let's go," Alex said, knowing precisely what was up.

They began to walk toward the pizzeria, which was half a mile from campus. Alex put his left hand in his pocket and offered the other one to Liam. Scott noticed that they were walking hand-in-hand, but he didn't say anything. Soon after they left campus, they saw the restaurant on the other side of the crossroad.

"Have you noticed that?" Scott asked and pointed to a gay nightclub near the restaurant.

"Um … no," Alex said with a blush.

"You should check it someday. The sign says the age limit is eighteen on Wednesdays and Thursdays," Scott said.

The club hadn't opened yet, and all Alex could see were the dark windows and the rainbow flags hanging on both sides of the entrance. It was the first gay club he had seen, as there were none in Fairmont.

They went to the pizzeria and ordered their food from the counter. Then they carried their drinks to an empty seat near the window, and soon, the waitress brought their steaming pizzas. The delicious smell of grease filled the air.

"How long have you guys been together?" Scott asked.

"We started dating just before our senior year," Liam said.

"I see. Don't tell me … you went to prom together," Scott said.

"Not exactly," Liam said, "but we did dance together there." He grinned.

"No shit? Two guys could've never danced in my high school in Texas," Scott said.

Alex stayed quiet and wondered if Scott agreed with that. He still wasn't sure what the big football player ultimately thought about him and Liam. Scott had been nothing but friendly toward them, but Alex couldn't help that the discussion about their relationship and prom dance made him uneasy.

"And you're out to your parents?" Scott asked, looking this time at Alex.

"Huh? No," Alex said, feeling even more uncomfortable. "I mean, Liam's parents are cool, but mine don't know."

"Sorry, man. It's really not my business," Scott said.

They continued eating their pizzas, and for a while, none of them said anything. The silence magnified the other noises. Alex heard the hiss of the soda fountain, the squeak of the bathroom door, and the murmur of conversations all around them. And all that was in his mind was the question of what Scott thought about him and Liam.

"I think my younger brother is like you," Scott said. "You know, gay."

"Why do you think so?" Liam asked.

"I don't know. It's just a feeling," Scott said and thought for a while. "I guess all his friends are girls, but they are just friends, and he's a bit … how should I say this…? A bit feminine or something."

"Oh," Liam said.

"Sorry. I didn't mean you were feminine," Scott said. "And I hate stereotyping people anyways."

Alex looked at the jock that was sitting opposite him. Scott played on the defensive line, which didn't come as a surprise. He was a rough guy, but the way he talked about his brother contradicted his stern appearance.

"What would you think about it if he were gay?" Alex asked.

"I hate how he's been bullied at school," Scott said, not really answering the question. "I'm afraid it's just going to get worse without me there to defend him."

"How about your parents? Can they talk to the principal or something?" Liam asked.

"If Shawn doesn't feel comfortable coming out to me, I don't think he'll talk to our folks either," Scott said.

It wasn't hard for Alex to understand that. If he had been bullied at high school for being gay—and, technically speaking, he had been—he wouldn't have told his parents. On the contrary, it had pushed him deeper into the closet with well-known results. He looked at Liam, who was still standing beside him despite all the horrible things he had done.

"I'm so lucky to have him," Alex said and took hold of his boyfriend's hand under the table. He was becoming more and more convinced that Scott didn't have a problem with him and Liam dating.

"Oh, you are so cute together," Scott said, wiping away Alex's last doubt. "I wish Shawn would find someone, too," he added, and his face grew serious.

A couple of weeks later, Alex walked into the shower room after his swim club meeting. The hall was a bit bigger than the one where he had practiced in high school, but otherwise, everything felt familiar.

"Good job, Wesley," Tyler said and patted Alex on his shoulder.

Tyler had received a scholarship to the university's team and had had a practice there almost every day over the past two weeks. The swim club gathered only twice a week. Since the swimming hall was big enough, they swam there at the same time with the varsity athletes.

"Nothing compared to you," Alex said, and he meant it. He had seen what a talented athlete Tyler was, and although Alex had been disappointed at not getting a scholarship, he understood the reason now.

"Not everybody can be like me," Tyler said and flashed a smile. "You need to work on those muscles," he added, squeezing Alex's biceps.

Alex laughed but felt a little off that the naked athlete was standing so close to him and touching him.

Despite being worried that his body would react to the closeness, he was pleased that Tyler didn't seem to care that he was gay. Not all had been so open-minded on his swimming team in high school.

"Do you want to join me in the gym tomorrow, or do you have other plans with your boyfriend?" Tyler asked.

Alex blushed. Many of the swimmers were still there taking showers, and even though Alex wasn't hiding his relationship with Liam anymore, he hadn't told the others either. Seeing Alex's face, Tyler realized what he had done, and the expression on his face was beyond apologetic.

"Sure. We don't have any plans," Alex said as casually as he could.

"You have a boyfriend? Liam?" Elyo asked. He was a short guy whose parents were Filipinos.

"Um … yeah, we're dating," Alex said.

"Cool," Elyo said as he continued washing his black hair.

Elyo and Alex were both computer engineering majors, and since they both had joined the swim club, they had started to become friends. Elyo knew that Alex shared a dorm room with Liam, but Alex had never mentioned that they were an item.

Only when Alex was walking toward the dorm did he realize that Tyler had outed him in the showers, but none of the guys had said a word. They all continued talking to him and washing themselves like nothing had happened. *You are no longer in high school*, Alex reminded himself.

"Alex!" Tyler shouted. Alex turned and saw Tyler running toward him.

"I'm sorry about what I said," Tyler panted. "Scott saw you kissing Liam in the park, and I thought they knew."

"It's okay."

"So, we're good?"

"Sure."

As Tyler flashed a smile and then jogged toward his dorm, Alex couldn't help but stare at his butt for a while before he opened the front door of his own building. Tyler was hot, but even hotter was his cute boyfriend who was waiting for him in bed. In seconds, Alex had stripped and joined Liam under the blanket, covering him with kisses.

On the following Saturday, Alex and Liam spent time walking together in the big park near campus. There were plenty of other students and people who lived in the neighborhood enjoying the sun. These were the last days of September, and everybody expected autumn to come soon, bringing cold and rainy weather.

Alex took hold of Liam's hand, even though they were off campus. Liam smiled at his boyfriend, who looked gorgeous in the tight shirt and light-blue jeans. Their gazes met, and Liam saw confidence in Alex's blue eyes.

"I like this," Liam said cheerfully. "Holding your hand," he added and squeezed Alex's hand.

"I thought you would," Alex said, smiling.

An older couple approached them from the opposite direction. When their paths crossed, the man gave them a disapproving look. Liam heard him saying something to his wife, but he didn't catch the words. A bit concerned, he glanced at Alex.

"They seemed to have problem with us walking hand-in-hand," Alex said casually.

"We don't have to do this," Liam said hesitantly. "I mean, if it makes you feel uncomfortable."

Alex stopped and took hold of Liam's other hand, too. He smiled and planted a kiss on Liam's lips. A broad smile appeared on Liam's face, and his brown eyes were twinkling with mirth.

"I like that smile," Alex said. "It's one of the things that made me fall for you."

Liam was speechless. He recalled the Alex who, during his senior year at high school, was too scared to go to a restaurant with him. A lot had happened after that, and Liam liked it.

"Besides, I don't feel uncomfortable being with you," Alex said. "Not anymore," he added, knowing that in high school things had been different. Luckily, they were no longer there.

As they kept walking, they caught some odd looks occasionally, but they ignored them and focused on each other. Soon, they came to a larger clearing where people were lying on the grass. They decided to sit down there, too, and soon Alex lay down, pulling Liam so close to him that his head was resting on Alex's chest.

"I think we should send a thank you card to Mr. Timothy," Alex said, think about how their high school history teacher had brought them together by asking them to prepare a presentation for the class.

"Yeah, we should," Liam agreed. That day, when Alex had been assigned to be his partner, had been one of the highlights of his junior year.

"And now we are here. Who would have thought?" Alex said and turned Liam's face toward his so that they could kiss. Liam's lips were soft and tasted of love.

As they were in no hurry to be anywhere, they kept lying on the grass, talking and kissing. For the first time, Alex felt completely free. Holding his cute and kind boyfriend close to him, he hoped that this moment would last forever.

But, like many good things in his life, it didn't.

Chapter 4

It was the first Saturday of October, and autumn recess would last until Wednesday. Alex and Liam had woken up early, but they had been avoiding talking to each other while cleaning their room. They had to make sure that nothing in the room gave the slightest hint that they were more than roommates.

"I need a shower," Liam said as he took off his dirty, sweaty shirt.

Alex muttered something as a reply. He hadn't been sleeping much, which was now causing him an awful headache. It didn't make him feel any better that his parents would be there within a couple of hours. It was the first time he would see them since he'd left Fairmont at the end of August.

Liam left for the showers, slamming the door behind him. Alex wasn't sure whether it was just an accident or if Liam had done it on purpose. Maybe his boyfriend was pissed off because he had pulled their beds apart the previous night. Alex couldn't explain why, but somehow he had been afraid that his parents would take them by surprise while they were still sleeping.

Is there still something that could expose us? Alex wondered, scanning the room one more time. He found nothing. They had even split the groceries in the fridge to make it look like both of them had their own compartments there. It was ridiculous, and Alex was sure his mother wouldn't even look inside the fridge.

"Your turn, roommate," Liam said when he returned to their room.

"That's unfair. You know how my parents would take it if they found out about us."

Liam studied Alex for a moment and then sighed. He hugged his boyfriend, and they kissed. Soon, small, compassionate smiles appeared on both of their faces.

"I'm sorry," Liam said. "I just don't like this acting. It makes me feel like there's something wrong with me."

"I don't like it either," Alex said.

"It's really not your fault," Liam said, annoyed at the situation but feeling embarrassed that he had put it all down to Alex.

Alex took a shower, and they ate breakfast in their room. It was still more than an hour before Alex's parents would arrive, so they decided to go out and walk in the park. This time, they didn't hold hands or kiss. They just walked there silently.

When they were walking back, Liam saw Mr. and Mrs. Wesley stepping out of their car in a nearby parking space. They were dressed as formally as he had expected, especially Alex's mother.

"Hi, honey. How are you?" Mrs. Wesley said as she hugged her son.

"Um … I'm okay. Nice to see you," Alex said. A part of him meant it; the other part was not so sure.

Mr. Wesley patted his son on the shoulder. Then he turned to look at Liam, who offered his hand to him and his wife. Both of them shook Liam's hand, and Mrs. Wesley was even interested in hearing how his studies had progressed. Alex watched tensely as his boyfriend explained what a fantastic history program Eastwood University had.

They went into the building where their dorm room was and walked to the second floor. Mrs. Wesley looked around the lobby and saw a group of couches and a TV in one corner. The expression on her face told Liam that she found the atmosphere a bit vulgar for her son. She didn't have time to comment before they heard someone walking down the stairs. It was Tyler, who had stopped by to visit a friend on the third floor.

Please don't say anything stupid, Alex prayed inwardly when Tyler approached them. He was absolutely cool about Alex and Liam being a couple. Alex hoped he would not be too cool and mention it to his parents.

"Hi, guys," Tyler said, "and you must be … Alex's parents?"

"That's right," Alex said.

"Nice to meet you, Mr. and Mrs. Wesley. Your son is a talented swimmer," Tyler said and shook their hands. "I'm Tyler, by the way."

"Oh, you are the swimmer Alex mentioned," Mrs. Wesley said, smiling at him.

"Yeah, I'm the famous and handsome one," Tyler said and smirked. "Not that Alex has ever called me handsome," he added once he realized what he had said.

The clarification didn't make it sound any better, and Alex closed his eyes, wishing that the situation would end. Luckily, Tyler understood that he should leave. He was a funny guy, and Alex liked him a lot. It was just that sometimes he had a bit too big of a mouth.

"Should we go in?" Alex said and opened the door to their room.

"This reminds me of my first dorm room," his father said.

Liam took a seat on his bed and picked up a book from the table, pretending to be searching for something. Mr. and Mrs. Wesley stood on the other side of the room and looked around. They all seemed to be having difficulties finding something to say.

"So, this is where you live," Mrs. Wesley said to Alex.

"Yeah, this is our home now," Alex said and immediately regretted that he had called it their home instead of his room. *Did it sound like we are a couple?*

Apparent, his parents hadn't thought so. Instead, they told Alex that they had made reservations at a nice restaurant, and they should leave soon. Alex considered his options briefly before deciding to ask if Liam could join them.

"But darling," Mrs. Wesley said politely but firmly, "your roommate will understand for sure that it's a family lunch."

"Of course," Liam said quickly. "Don't worry about me. I'll eat on campus."

"Okay then. I need to change clothes," Alex said. "Um … could you wait outside?"

The dorm room was one space, and he didn't want to strip in front of his parents. Alex's mother followed her husband out of the room. She kept the door open for Liam until she realized that he would stay. Both Mr. and Mrs. Wesley became aware that Liam would be there watching whenever their son took off his clothes, but they forced themselves not to think about it.

"I'm sorry that you can't come with us," Alex said, putting his hands on his boyfriend's shoulders. He hoped that Liam wouldn't be hurt.

"Don't worry," Liam said. "I can only imagine how awkward it would be, me sitting there with your parents," he added with a smirk.

Alex had to admit that Liam was probably right. They hugged and then kissed. If Alex's parents hadn't been waiting behind the door, they would have been fooling around in their bed before much longer. Reluctantly, Alex let go of Liam and changed clothes.

Soon, Alex was sitting in the backseat of his father's car, sad that Liam couldn't join them. He had promised his cute and kind boyfriend that, as soon as they moved to Eddington, he would tell the whole world how happy and proud he was to have Liam beside him. And now, how bittersweet it was that his own parents forced him back into the closet, where he felt ashamed of who he was.

"How has it been … living with Liam?" his mother asked.

"It's cool. Nice to live with someone I know rather than some total stranger," Alex said, guessing where this discussion was leading.

"He hasn't been touching you or anything?" she asked.

"Mom!" Alex protested. *Yes, we have been touching each other in every possible way almost every night, and I fucking love it*, Alex thought.

"Sorry, darling. I just wanted to know that everything was all right for you."

"Couldn't be better," Alex said, pretty sure that his mother missed the sarcastic tone in his voice.

Mr. Wesley parked the car in front of the restaurant, and they walked in. The waiter guided them to the table and brought their menus. It was an Italian restaurant, far too expensive for Alex's student budget. If his parents were trying to make an impression on him, they weren't too successful.

All the feelings of rejection kept flashing in Alex's mind. He remembered how heartbroken he had been after Rick had forced him to date that girl and Liam had left him as a result. He had even lost count of how many times he had denied Liam and their relationship. And the reasons for all this were sitting in front of him.

Am I a bad person if I hate my parents? Alex thought as a teardrop appeared in the corner of his eye.

"Are you okay?" Mrs. Wesley asked.

"Yeah. I'm just happy to see you," Alex lied and swiped the teardrop from his cheek.

"Alex, men don't cry," his father said.

Luckily, the waiter brought their food, allowing Alex to think about something else. The pasta was good. Actually, it was delicious, but that didn't change the fact that he would prefer to spend the day on campus with Liam.

"Alex, your father and I have a surprise for you," Mrs. Wesley said after they had finished eating and the waiter had collected their plates.

"Huh? What is it?" Alex said, baffled.

"I'm renting you an apartment off-campus," she said and smiled like a small girl seeing her pony for the first time.

"What? Freshmen have to live on campus," Alex said. *Besides, I want to live with Liam.*

"My friend knows the Dean. I'm sure you will get an exception considering your living conditions," she said.

"What living conditions?" Alex snapped.

"Your roommate is homosexual. It's not normal," Mr. Wesley said. His voice was quiet, but only because he didn't want the other customers to hear how his son was living.

Alex was breathing heavily. His brain was overloaded from all he had just heard and thinking about how to reply to his father. At the same time, he knew that, if he lost his cool, he could say goodbye to the funding that his parents were giving him.

"Liam is my friend, and I—" Alex began to say.

"We pay your tuition, so we expect you to respect the decision we've made," Mrs. Wesley said.

Alex sighed. Apparently, his parents had made up their minds, and even from hundreds of miles away, they could still control his life.

"Darling, would you like some dessert?" Mrs. Wesley asked.

"No thanks, I'm fine," Alex said. *The sooner I get out of here, the better.*

"Okay, let's get you back to the university," Mr. Wesley said, "and then I guess it's time for us to start heading back home." He looked at his wife, who nodded as a response.

The journey back to campus was silent. As soon as they got there, Alex opened the back door, thanked his parents for the ride and lunch, and rushed to his dorm room, which was empty. Hoping that Liam had just gone for lunch and wasn't mad at him, after all, Alex began to bemoan the situation. *My parents want me to move away from here. They don't want me to share a room with Liam. Fuck!*

Paul had been driving for four hours while Sara had tried to get some sleep. The front seat of Paul's black Audi was comfortable, but not comfortable enough for sleeping. Travelling twelve hours back and forth to see their son had sounded a better idea than it was.

"Are you tired? Should I drive for a while?" Sara asked.

"No, I'm fine," Paul said and kept looking at the highway in front of them.

"I wonder if everything is okay. Alex seemed a bit anxious, don't you think?" she said.

"Nah, he'll be all right. He just needs his own apartment," he said.

Sara looked at her husband, whose indifference was starting to annoy her. On the other hand, Sara hadn't told him what she had seen on the night of Alex's high school prom. Mostly, she had kept it to herself because not saying it aloud made it almost like it hadn't happened. After seeing them in their dorm room, she couldn't lie to herself anymore.

They had been sitting in the backyard, and Alex had wrapped his arm around that boy, she recalled the events of the night. Sara was sure that, in some way, Liam was now using her son.

She had done what every caring mother would do in that situation. One of her friends was a lawyer in Eddington, and she knew Samantha Curtis. Sara had written an exception application, and her friend had promised to talk about it to Dean Curtis personally. With all these preparations, it should be a piece of cake for Alex to get permission to live off-campus.

Actually, Sara had been so sure about her plan that she had already started the arrangements to rent an apartment near Eastwood University. The real estate agent had sent information about some promising places. It was unfortunate that she hadn't had a chance to show them to Alex. The boy had been too stubborn.

"You're thinking about something," Paul said. "You have that look on your face."

"It's nothing. Work issues," Sara said.

"Try to get some sleep. You look tired," Paul said.

Sara tried, but every time she closed her eyes, she saw Alex and Liam sitting in the backyard and looking at each other just like they were about to kiss. Finally, she was able to get some sleep, and when she woke up, they were almost at home—and she had quite a headache.

"Drive me to the hospital," she said, holding her head in pain.

"Are you okay?" Paul asked, even though he knew she wasn't.

"My head … can't see … help me," Sara was able to say before she passed out.

Paul turned the car toward the hospital and took his phone from his pocket. Dialing 9-1-1, he drove as fast as he could. Since they were only a couple of miles from the hospital, the calm officer on the other side of the line instructed him to continue and promised to make sure that they were ready at the hospital to take care of her.

"She was holding her head and said that she couldn't see," Paul explained to the emergency unit staff waiting for them. His voice was more angry than fearful.

"Please, stay alive," he said to his wife, who looked so small and fragile on the stretcher.

Paul waited in the hall, looking at the doctors and nurses who were running here and there. Now and then, the door was opened, and a new patient was brought in. It took ages, and still, nobody seemed to know what had happened to his wife.

Finally, a young woman approached him and introduced herself as Dr. Jenkins. Paul looked at her like a convict waiting to hear the length of his sentence.

"Your wife was suffering from a rise in pressure of the cerebrospinal fluid, which affected the cerebral cortex and caused the headache and decreased consciousness," she said.

"Can I have that in English, please?" Paul said.

"There is fluid circulating in her brain," she explained slowly. "We gave her medicine to lower the pressure of that fluid back to normal," she added.

"So, she's alive?" Paul asked.

"Oh. Sorry, I forgot to mention that she's fine, and you can meet her now," she said and looked embarrassed.

Paul followed the doctor to the room where they had taken his wife. Sara was pale, but in Paul's eyes, she was still the beautiful Sara he had fallen in love with twenty years ago. They hugged for a long time.

"Thank God you're okay! I was so worried," Paul said.

Sara gave him a small smile, but something in her look put Paul on alert. He looked at the doctor, who gestured for him to sit down. Apparently, everything was not okay. Paul wasn't sure if he wanted to hear more, but it seemed to be inevitable.

"The increased pressure is a symptom of something," the doctor said. "We have now treated the symptom, but we still need to find the cause."

"Is it a tumor? Is she gonna die?" Paul asked, looking at the doctor with his desperate eyes.

"A tumor is one possible cause, however quite unlikely," she said.

"What is it then?" Paul said.

"We need to run tests before I can answer that," she said. "We'll be a lot wiser on Monday afternoon."

Reluctantly, and after several goodbyes, Paul left his wife at the hospital and drove home. He pondered whether to call Alex, but decided that he didn't want to worry him before they knew more. It was better to let Alex relax and enjoy his autumn recess.

It had been a long day for Paul, and he was tired. He went to bed knowing that he couldn't sleep well until he knew what was wrong with his wife. Monday afternoon was painfully far in the future.

They were all looking at him and waiting for him to start. It was Monday morning, and Paul was standing in front of his employees. His hands were shaking, and he gave a nervous smile to those who were standing in the front row.

"I have some bad news," he said.

There was no reaction from the audience. They just kept staring at him like chicks waiting for their mother bird to bring some worms.

"The head office is not satisfied with our financial performance, and they have asked me to reduce our number of employees," Paul said.

"Are we going to be fired?" one of his senior employees asked.

"Unfortunately, they didn't give me a choice," Paul said.

Technically speaking, his boss had not asked him to lay off people. He had just asked Paul to improve sales without sacrificing the margin. However, Paul found it easier to blame the leadership of Henderson Watson Sport.

"How am I supposed to pay my mortgage if I lose my job?" another employee asked.

"This situation is very unfortunate—" Paul began to say.

"Of course it is! I don't give a shit," the employee said.

"Let's all calm down," Paul said and felt how his armpits were sweating.

"Just let us know who's going to be fired!" someone shouted.

"Fine. Fair enough," Paul said. "I'll pass out the pink slips by lunch time."

Having said that, he thanked them and returned to his office. He hadn't expected such a reaction from his employees. They had been like a family, and Paul had done so much to make sure that they were satisfied. *Selfish idiots*, he thought and reviewed the termination notices one more time.

"Hi, Paul. Quite a Monday morning," Alma Hanson said when Paul entered her office.

"It wasn't easy to give that kind of news," Paul said, looking for her sympathy.

"You did it well," Alma said.

"Thanks," Paul said and sat down.

"So, I assume you wanted to talk about my team and who I need to let go?" Alma said.

Paul looked at his best friend's wife, and all those hard times when Tommy had supported him flashed through his mind. He hoped that what he would do next would not ruin their friendship.

"Alma, actually, I—" Paul began, but Alma interrupted him.

"Aha, you've already made the decision. I hope Kenny can stay. He's done a very good job," she said.

"Kenny stays, and he'll replace you," Paul blurted out. "I'm sorry," he added and stood up.

"So, that's it? I'm fired?" Alma said when Paul's message started to sink in.

"That's it," Paul said and left the room. Alma was on the verge of tears, and he couldn't watch it.

It hardly took more than fifteen minutes for Paul to distribute the rest of the pink slips. Most of the people just took the paper and left. After the last employee had received his notice, Paul climbed to the second-floor balcony and looked at the store. He saw apathetic people here and there preparing to open the doors for customers. The smile on their faces had disappeared.

Paul's phone started to ring, and he hoped and feared that it was from the hospital. It wasn't. The caller was Mr. Brownlee.

"Morning, sir," Paul answered the phone.

"How are you progressing?" Mr. Brownlee asked.

"Fine, sir," Paul said quickly. "I'm sure you will see positive development in the Christmas sales or at the latest during the first quarter next year," he added.

"Paul, I'm not going to wait that long," Mr. Brownlee said.

"But, sir—"

"No buts, Paul. Don't put me in a position that I need to start looking for a new store manager."

"No, sir. I'll do my best."

The line went dead, and Paul wasn't even sure if Mr. Brownlee had heard his last sentence. In fact, it didn't matter. It was starting to look like Mr. Brownlee had already made a decision to replace him. Now, the son-of-a-bitch was just trying to put pressure on him so that he would leave voluntarily without the severance payment written in his contract.

Paul heard music coming from the speakers, and one of his employees opened the roll-down gate in front of the main door. It was ten o'clock and time to open the store. Paul waited twenty minutes monitoring the door, but only two customers came in.

I'm screwed, Paul thought and left the building using the back door. It was better to let the employees calm down. He had done what he was forced to do, and now his staff seemed to be mad at him. Besides, he had other things to worry about. Sara was still in the hospital, and he hadn't heard anything about the test results.

Paul decided to drive to the hospital. Maybe they had some good news that would cheer him up. Feeling hopeful, he stepped into his car without noticing that some of the employees he had just fired had scratched the paint on the left back door.

When he got to the hospital, he rushed to the room where his wife had been the previous night when he left for home. Sara was there with Dr. Jenkins, whose face was deadly serious. Paul looked at his wife and saw her crying. She must have gotten the test results.

"What is it?" Paul asked and heard his voice cracking.

The answer was like someone had thrown a bucket of cold water on him. No, it was even worse.

Chapter 5

Shawn Abrahamson was standing in front of a small store half a mile from his high school, just as he had done many times over the past two weeks. It was their secret meeting place, and even though people driving along Lake Austin Boulevard might see him, his classmates rarely hung around there.

He didn't have to wait long before he spotted Jamal crossing the road. *He's so handsome*, Shawn thought and smiled unconsciously.

They had met each other in a discussion forum on the internet, and if Shawn had counted right, this was the seventh time they had met in person. Like Shawn, Jamal was a high school senior, but they went to different high schools.

"Hi," Shawn said shyly.

Jamal responded to his greeting. They didn't hug even though both of them wanted to. Shawn's heart was beating faster, and he was nervous. Jamal was the first boy he had ever dated, and the first to whom he had come out.

"What did your parents say? Did you tell them?" Jamal asked.

Shawn shook his head and looked embarrassed. He and Jamal had sat on the grass behind the parking area the day before and talked about his plan to tell his parents that he was gay. Jamal had wished him good luck, and Shawn, packed with confidence, had driven home where his parents had been sitting in the kitchen. He had opened his mouth, but a simple "hello" was all that had come out.

"I'm gonna try again today," Shawn said, feeling optimistic that he would be more successful this time.

"It's a big decision," Jamal said with his soft voice. "Once you have said it, you can't take it back."

"Yup," Shawn said.

They sat in silence for a while, which was very unusual for Shawn. Normally, he was talking all the time. As most of his friends at high school were girls, he had learned to open his mouth and take his place. If he stayed silent waiting for his turn, it would never come.

With Jamal, it was different. The boy smiled a lot but talked only when he had something important on his mind, like he had to pay for every word he said. Shawn loved those silent moments. He loved everything about Jamal.

"How's your grandma?" Shawn asked.

Jamal's parents had died in an accident when he was three years old, and since then, he had been living with his grandparents. Unfortunately, his grandfather had passed away two years earlier. It was just Jamal and his sixty-eight-year-old grandmother living in their big house.

"Getting better," Jamal said. "Wasn't coughing too much last night so I got some sleep," he added with a smirk.

God, I love those white teeth, those light blue eyes and that short, curly hair, Shawn thought, looking at his new friend and pondering whether he could call Jamal his boyfriend already.

"She doesn't know you like boys?" Shawn asked, even though he remembered Jamal mentioning something about it.

"No, she's too old. She wouldn't understand," Jamal said, but he didn't look sad.

They watched the cars driving along Lake Austin Boulevard and turning up the ramp that merged with the South MoPac Expressway. Austin was one of the fastest-growing metropolises in the U.S. On the other hand, Jamal had said that the percentage of black people had dropped from twenty-five to eight percent and was still decreasing. Shawn found Jamal's interest in numbers and details cute, although that particular statistic meant that Jamal was one of very few African-Americans in the city.

"Let's walk to the bridge over the river," Shawn said. "I can drive you near your house later."

"Sure, it's beautiful there," Jamal agreed. He looked at Shawn's nicely-tanned, narrow face, and long, light-brown hair, which almost hid his green eyes. His eye color was rare, especially for a male, but Jamal liked it.

It took them less than ten minutes to walk to the pedestrian bridge, which was also known as the Roberta Crenshaw Pedestrian Walkway. They walked halfway across the bridge and looked east, but couldn't see Shawn's school behind the trees. Austin High School was the oldest public high school in the city.

Jamal's high school was eight miles north, and it had taken over an hour for him to travel by bus to get near Shawn's school. Usually, he would drive there in his car, but he had dropped it off for some maintenance that morning and wouldn't get it back before Monday.

"Unbelievable," Shawn said. "I still can't believe you took the bus here."

"I wanted to see you," Jamal said and gave Shawn a broad smile. "Besides, my school day finished an hour earlier than yours, so I had plenty of time."

"Well, I hope I can bring you to my home soon," Shawn said.

"That sounds serious."

"Do you mind if it sounds serious?"

"I'm cool with that."

They looked each other in the eyes, and then Shawn moved his gaze to Jamal's lips. He took a step closer, gathering the courage to kiss the boy. Jamal did nothing to stop him, but before their lips touched each other, Shawn backed off. He wasn't brave enough to do it after all.

Realizing what had happened, Jamal smiled at Shawn to let him know that he was okay. They were in a public place, and even though Austin was a rather liberal city, neither of them were ready to take the step. As long as they were just walking and talking, people around them perceived them as friends, not boyfriends.

"Would you like to go to a movie tomorrow?" Shawn asked.

"Like a date?" Jamal said.

Shawn nodded and blushed slightly. It was the first time he had asked another boy out in person. Jamal had just traveled over an hour to meet him, but Shawn was still worried that he would say no.

"I would love that," Jamal said with his soft voice, which made him sound sexy to Shawn.

He likes me! Shawn rejoiced, and the expression on his face was so obvious that Jamal didn't have any trouble guessing what he was thinking. The feeling was mutual.

They talked for half an hour, standing on the bridge and enjoying the sunny weather, and then they began to walk toward Shawn's school. Once again, Shawn reminded himself of his decision to come out to his parents today and felt nervous about their reaction. To Scott, he wouldn't say a word; his brother was a jock and would not understand.

Shawn's car was on the other side of the parking area, and they ran into Oliver and Jake on their way there. In Shawn's evaluation scale, those two boys held the highest degree of being morons. He tried to ignore them, but Oliver wasn't going to miss the opportunity to give Shawn a hard time.

"Hi, gaylord. Is that jungle bunny your new girlfriend?" Oliver said with a venomous smile on his face.

"Whatever you say," Shawn said and started to walk faster. Jamal followed him without saying a word.

Oliver yelled something, but Shawn didn't want to listen to him. Luckily, Oliver and Jake continued in the other direction, and Shawn and Jamal were able to walk to Shawn's car without further interruptions.

"Sorry about that," Shawn said as soon as they got inside his Ford Mondeo.

"No problem. Wasn't the first time I met idiots," Jamal said, and something in the way he said it convinced Shawn that Jamal had got his own share of shit, too. High schools were designed for popular and athletic kids, not for those like Shawn or Jamal.

After driving Jamal home, Shawn opened the front door of his house and heard his parents speaking in the living room. Dropping his bag on the floor, he went to the kitchen to take a soda pop from the fridge. He was nervous, but he was determined to do it now.

"Hi, sweetheart," his mother said as soon as Shawn appeared at the living room door.

"We were planning to meet Janet's family tomorrow. Would you like to join us?" Shawn's father asked.

Aunt Janet lived quite far away from Austin, and Shawn knew that the visit would take the whole day. He liked his father's sister, but visiting her would mean that

Shawn would have to cancel his date with Jamal, which was out of the question.

"Um, I have other plans. I'm meeting someone," he said.

"Aww, my baby has a date," his mother said enthusiastically.

Shawn blushed and knew that this was the moment. If he didn't say it now, the moment would be gone, and he would fail like he had the previous day. Shawn drew air into his lungs and expelled it through his mouth.

"I'm meeting another guy," Shawn blurted out.

"Does that meant that you are…?" his mother said.

"Gay," Shawn finished the sentence and nodded, waiting for his parents' reaction.

"It's okay, sweetheart. We love you," she said, smiling at Shawn. "To be honest, I can't say that I'm surprised."

If Shawn had expected some family drama, he didn't get it. Instead, he felt a huge burden lift from his shoulders. His heartbeat was returning to normal, and Shawn tried to hide his shaking hands behind his back.

So, that was it? Are we supposed to hug now? Shawn thought. He didn't have to wait long before his parents stood up from the sofa and wrapped their arms around him. Shawn tried to hold back his tears, but at least one drop managed to escape from his eye.

"Does your brother know?" Shawn's father asked once he had sat down again.

Shawn shook his head. "Please don't tell him," he said.

"Whoever you want to tell, it's your choice," his mother said.

Scott was a football player and had spent a significant part of his time at high school in the locker room with the other jocks. He was an athlete and popular, everything that Shawn wished to be but wasn't. Shawn was worried that he would lose what was left of his brother's respect if Scott knew that he was gay.

"We live in two different worlds. He wouldn't understand," Shawn said.

"Don't be so sure," his father said.

"No, he wouldn't," Shawn said to finish that part of the conversation.

His parents wanted to know more about Jamal and seemed pleased to hear that he was a senior at L.C. Anderson High School, located in northwest Austin. Shawn, for his part, was satisfied that his parents asked him to bring Jamal to their house someday. Introducing his boyfriend to his parents would be awkward, but at least they hadn't tried to force him back into the closet.

Shawn's mother found it sad that Jamal's parents had died so early that the boy couldn't even remember them. Jamal had been raised by his grandparents who had owned a prosperous real estate business, which his grandmother had sold after her husband had died.

"Are his grandparents Morgan and Norma King?" Shawn's father asked.

"Yes, how did you know that?" Shawn said, surprised.

"Their firm sold us this house," Shawn's father said. "I wouldn't be surprised if they were involved in closing every real estate deal in the neighborhood," he added.

Cool, I have a rich boyfriend. I should marry him quickly, Shawn thought and smiled at the idea.

Finally, it was Saturday evening, and Shawn had promised to pick up Jamal in half an hour. Frustrated, Shawn took the third shirt from his wardrobe and tried it on, seeing how it would look with his jeans in front of the mirror. Realizing that he would be late, he thought that it had to do.

Shawn was putting on the shirt when his phone began to ring. *It has to be Jamal*, he thought and answered the phone without looking at the screen.

"Hi baby, I'll be there soon," Shawn said.

"Um, why are you coming to Eddington?" his brother said.

"Scott, shit, I thought it was … someone else," Shawn said.

"Aww, my baby brother's got a date," Scott teased.

"Busted," Shawn said. "I met the girl at school."

The line was silent for a while. Just when Shawn was about to ask whether his brother was still there, Scott asked what they were planning to do.

"I'm taking her to the movies," Shawn said.

"Hopefully not some action flick," Scott said.

"Nah, a romantic comedy," Shawn said and looked at his watch. "But look, I need to go now so that we won't be late. Talk to you later. Okay?"

"Sure, have a nice evening."

There wasn't a lot of traffic, and it took twenty-five minutes for Shawn to drive to the meeting place near Jamal's house. He might have been a couple of minutes late, but Jamal didn't care. Most likely, he hadn't even noticed it. Flashing Shawn a broad smile, Jamal jumped into the car, and they drove downtown.

Shawn left his car in a parking garage on University Avenue, and they walked to the movie theater that was on the other side of Martin Luther King Jr. Boulevard. The sun had set, and the street lights illuminated the buildings. Shawn wanted to take hold of Jamal's hand, but neither of them was ready for it.

They entered the crowded hall and were happy that Shawn had bought the tickets upfront on the internet. After buying some soft drinks and popcorn, they went inside the big auditorium.

I'm on a date with this cool guy, Shawn thought and was sure that nothing could go wrong. Jamal was cute and kind, and Shawn realized that he was developing a serious crush on him. Maybe it wasn't that bad.

Just as Shawn was about to sit, he saw Oliver and Jake three rows behind them. They were with two girls, whom Shawn assumed to be juniors from their school. Oliver smiled at him, but Shawn was sure that it wasn't a friendly smile.

"Everything okay?" Jamal asked.

"Um, sure," Shawn said and forced the smile back on his face. He didn't want to let anyone ruin his date with Jamal.

Chapter 6

On Sunday morning, Alex and Liam slept in. Even after both of them had woken up, they were lying around in the beds that Alex had pushed together as soon as his parents had left for Fairmont.

"Mmm," Alex murmured when Liam crawled under his blanket.

Their naked bodies touched each other, and Alex was hard in a flash. Soon, he felt Liam's hand wrapping around his erection. *God, I love college,* he thought and did his best to enjoy the moment.

Alex hadn't told Liam yet that his parents were organizing an apartment so that they could not live together. The news would disappoint Liam, and Alex had been waiting for the right time since Liam got back to their room the previous afternoon. And this wasn't the perfect moment either.

Grinning mischievously, Liam turned his boyfriend on his side and moved up close behind him. Alex felt Liam's erection against his butt, and he knew what was going to happen next. He loved the intimate moment and the connection that it created between them. They were as close to each other as possible.

Liam had his arms wrapped around Alex's upper body, and it didn't take long for either of them to reach the point of no return.

"I love you so much," Alex said when they were both lying on their backs and panting.

The expression on Liam's face was so obvious that even a dumb jock could figure out that the feeling was mutual. At least, the kiss Liam planted on Alex's lips confirmed it.

"I need a shower," Alex said after they had been lying there another half an hour.

"Mmm … I would love to join you," Liam said, and his eyes had the twinkle that Alex loved.

"Um … that would be nice, but there may be others," Alex said. "He might be too eager to shower with you," he added and looked down at his crotch.

"I would be so happy to shower with him," Liam said, staring at Alex's penis, which started to swell.

"Stop it. You're making me hard again," Alex said, covering his crotch with his hands.

"Then it's maybe better that I take my shower first," Liam said and grabbed his towel. "You can clean the room in the meantime," he said before he left the room.

This was the Liam Alex loved. He wasn't only sweet and kind but also funny and stunningly cute. Alex decided to talk some sense into his mother. There was no way she could force them to move apart. Liam also deserved to know what his parents were planning.

"Liam. Um … I have something I need to tell you," Alex said when both of them had taken showers, and they were eating breakfast.

"What is it?" Liam said with a worried frown.

"Please, don't freak out. This sounds worse than it is," Alex said.

"Okay."

"My parents want me to move to an off-campus apartment."

"Strange, but I don't understand what's so bad about that," Liam said. Alex watched as realization dawned in Liam's eyes. "Wait … you're going to move there alone because they don't want their straight son to live with a gay guy?"

Alex nodded. That was how he assumed his parents perceived their current arrangement. Of course, from his parents' perspective, the reality was even worse. They were already on the edge, and there was no question whether all hell would break loose if they knew that Liam was, in fact, his boyfriend.

"Obviously, you're not going to move?" Liam put it as a question even though it was more like a statement.

"Um…," Alex hesitated, trying to decide what to say.

"What? Are you seriously even considering it?" Liam snapped. His cheeks started to redden out of anger.

"What fucking choice do I have?" Alex said, raising his voice, too. "They'll stop paying my tuition and everything if I don't do what they want."

Liam didn't say a word. He just stared at his boyfriend, and a massive wave of frustration went through his body.

"I fucking hate my parents. I wish they were dead," Alex said and swiped the box of cereal to the floor. The cornflakes flew all over the room.

Liam stood up and left the room. He sat on the couch in the lobby and wrapped his arms around his legs. He was mad at Alex and even more angry at Alex's parents. But most of all, it was the situation that made him feel frustrated. They hadn't done anything wrong, but life was still so unfair.

On Monday afternoon, Alex was sitting in his mandatory general chemistry class, trying to focus on the lecture. Unfortunately, his mind and heart were somewhere else, like they had been the whole day.

How am I going to convince Mom that I don't have to move without losing her financial support? he kept asking. He knew how stubborn she was after she had made her mind up. It was also clear that Liam was upset even though he had said that it wasn't Alex's fault.

Alex awoke from his thoughts when Tyler poked him in the arm.

"Mr. Wesley, would you mind answering the question?" the professor said.

"Uh … sorry, sir. What was the question again?" Alex asked, embarrassed.

"What are the unreactive nonmetals called?" the professor repeated the question.

"Alkali metals," Alex said. His voice was as diffident as when he had first asked Liam to be his boyfriend.

"Mr. Wesley, we are talking about nonmetals," the professor said, and a couple of students laughed a bit.

"Noble gasses," Tyler whispered to Alex at the same time as the teacher gave the correct answer.

In high school, Alex had been pretty good in chemistry. Unfortunately, the growing friction with his lab partner and former best friend had led to his hating the subject. Even here, every time he entered the class, he was reminded of Rick.

Five minutes before class ended, Professor Taylor started to return the thermochemistry essays back to the students. Alex felt anxious. Given the enormous amount of homework most of the teachers were giving him, he had finished his paper at the very last moment. Besides, he wasn't good at writing essays on any topic, and if he was asked, Professor Taylor wasn't an excellent teacher either.

"I think this is all for today. Mr. Wesley, would you mind staying for a short time?" the professor said as soon as he had given the papers back to everybody else except Alex.

Alex sat in his seat and looked at the other students who were leaving the classroom. Tyler gave him a small smile, which Alex considered as a friendly gesture. Professor Taylor's face was not as sympathetic when he approached with Alex's essay on his hand.

"Mr. Wesley, I'm afraid your essay doesn't give a very convincing picture of your understanding about the topic," the professor said.

"I was quite busy when I was writing it," Alex said, and it sounded like a lousy excuse even to him.

"The number of spelling mistakes made that quite evident," the professor said. Alex was able to hear the sarcastic tone in his voice.

The professor had a point, however. Alex couldn't say that he had fully understood the concepts of enthalpy and internal energy. Because of that, his essay about spontaneous endothermic reactions had been rather cursory, even in his own opinion. Apparently, Professor Taylor had found several mistakes in it, too.

I can't just tell him that he's a lousy teacher, Alex thought. He couldn't understand why software engineering students had to study chemistry in the first place.

"I've spoken with the teaching assistant," the professor said. "She said that your answers to the weekly exercises are often insufficient."

In addition to the lectures, the course consisted of mandatory exercises that the students were supposed to complete every week. Every Wednesday morning, there was a group session where the teaching assistant explained the correct solutions. Alex had thought that it was enough to drop his answers to the mailbox in the chemistry department. He was surprised to learn that the TA actually checked the papers.

"I hope you understand that, if you don't pass the course, you'll have to take it again next semester," the professor said.

Well, if you didn't know, that's the case for all mandatory courses, Alex thought but just nodded. At the end of the day, the professor was right, of course.

"I promise to try harder," Alex said for lack of a better response.

"You'd better, Mr. Wesley," the professor said. "I'll consider your essay passed, but you need to brush up quite a lot to pass the final exam," he added and gave Alex his paper.

Once the professor had left, Alex looked at his essay and noticed that it contained more red ink than his own handwriting. Frustrated, he folded it and put it in his bag. Then he headed to the swimming hall.

Two hours later, Liam and Scott were waiting for their roommates in front of the swimming hall. Alex had promised to drive them to the mall, and Tyler would join them, too. Even though he was dating one, Liam was surprised that many of his best friends at the college were jocks.

"How's your brother?" Liam asked Scott.

"I called on Saturday, and he told me he has a girlfriend," Scott said.

"Oh … okay."

"Uh huh, that was my reaction as well."

What Scott was saying didn't fit into the picture that his little brother was gay and being bullied, unless there was another logical explanation. Liam was pretty sure what it would be.

"Could he date some girl just to pretend to be straight?" Liam asked. "To get rid of those who are harassing him?"

"That's possible. Actually, I was thinking that, too."

"That would only make him more depressed," Liam said. "Trust me. I know from experience," he added before he realized what he had just said.

"You've dated a girl, too?" Scott asked, raising his eyebrows.

Liam wasn't sure what to say. He had been talking about Alex, whose suicide attempt he had witnessed that horrible night he tried to forget. Liam wanted to help Scott's brother, but it wasn't his job to share what his boyfriend had gone through.

"Not me, but Alex," Liam said quietly.

"Could I ask Alex to talk to Shawn?" Scott said.

"Uh … I would prefer if you didn't mention what I just told you to Alex," Liam said, embarrassed to take away the hope that he had just seen in Scott's eyes.

"I understand. I won't say a word," Scott said, hiding his disappointment.

It didn't take long before Alex and Tyler walked out of the swimming hall. Alex approached Liam, who wasn't sure what would happen next. They had hardly spoken to each other after Alex had told him about his plan to move off-campus.

To his pleasant surprise, Alex wrapped his arms around Liam and hugged him. Neither of them said anything since Tyler and Scott were standing beside them, but both of them felt that the argument was forgotten and forgiven.

"Let's go, lovebirds, before you make me so jealous that I start hugging Scott," Tyler said.

"Go ahead. We're not homophobic," Liam said and planted a kiss on Alex's lips.

"Eww, my superior masculinity would stand a hug, but kissing is so off-limits," Scott said.

Tyler laughed and made an attempt to kiss Scott, who took a couple of steps back. Liam smiled at their play, and then the four of them began walking toward the parking area. They had just spotted Alex's red Mustang when his phone started to ring.

"It's Dad," Alex said and considered a moment whether to answer. Finally, he rejected the call. He didn't feel like talking to him right now.

The phone started to ring again, and Alex pressed the red button once more. Tyler looked at him and was about to say something when the phone began to ring for the third time. Apparently, Mr. Wesley didn't want to give up that easily. Alex sighed and answered the call.

"Alex, so good that you answered," his dad slurred.

"Dad, are you drunk?" Alex asked.

"That's possible, but it's not the point. It's your mother."

"What about Mom?"

"She's dying."

Mr. Wesley sounded like he had been drinking the whole afternoon. Over and over again, Alex had to ask his father to repeat what he had said. Ultimately, Alex was able to connect the dots between the different pieces of the story his father was trying to tell him.

When the call was over, he was just staring at the screen.

"Mom has a brain tumor. She has only a couple of months left," Alex said finally and looked at Liam. Then his eyes started to fill with tears.

Chapter 7

Paul Wesley sat on the couch and watched TV. To be precise, he was more interested in the bottle of beer he was holding in his hand than the TV program. Either way, he had lost count how many beers he had drank and didn't know the name of the TV show either.

The doorbell rang. Once, twice, and then a third time. *Who the hell could that be?* Paul thought as he stood up. Walking toward the sound, he was able to find the hall and even got the door open.

"Alex," he said, blinking at his son who was standing there in the rain.

"Where's Mom?" Alex demanded, ignoring the fact that his father was drunk.

"She'll be in Heaven soon."

"Dad, seriously!"

"She's at Fairmont Memorial Hospital."

Alex seemed to be surprised by the answer. Paul couldn't blame his son for that. His wife was a lawyer in a big law firm. Surely, she would have had insurance that had covered treatment in the best hospitals in the country. They didn't even have a department of oncology at the community hospital.

"Mom is there because nothing can be done," Alex said, more to himself than his father.

"Palliative care," Paul did his best to pronounce the words correctly. "That's how they call it."

Taking the last sip from the bottle, Paul watched as Alex sat down on the floor and tears began to fall from his eyes. Irritated that his son had become such a wimp, Paul walked to the kitchen to get a new bottle of beer. *Real men don't cry*, he thought and felt the anger inside him growing.

Paul looked out of the window and saw Alex's red Mustang. He and Sara had bought it for Alex as a birthday present. It was a gift to a son who was supposed to become a top athlete. Now his wife was dying, and Alex hadn't even made it on the university's team. All his dreams were fading away.

"Can we go see Mom?" Alex asked from the kitchen door.

"You go. I don't want to see her," Paul said.

"But she's your wife. You can't abandon Mom just like that. She needs you."

"Don't you dare lecture me, boy."

Seeking a knife or something else to fight with, Paul started to move toward Alex, who realized that it was better to leave. Even in his current condition, Paul was a strong man. Luckily, he wasn't very fast, and Alex managed to run to his car before Paul reached the front door.

Paul saw the red Mustang reversing to the road. Then it was gone. He was sure that soon the car would be parked in front of Fairmont Memorial Hospital. He had been there the previous day, and it would be the last time.

In his most precious memories, Sara was that beautiful college girl he'd had a major crush on since the first time they saw each other at a party. She was a strong, independent woman, something that Paul had needed beside him over the years. That was how Paul wanted to remember her. Not as a gray and fragile shadow of what she had once been.

Feeling some embarrassment that he had evicted Alex, Paul returned to the living room. He was all alone again. He switched off the television, but the silence didn't last long as his phone started to ring almost simultaneously.

"Hello, Mr. Brownlee," Paul answered.

"Are you drunk?" Mr. Brownlee asked.

"Yay, you're a smart guy, Mr. Brownlee," Paul said, thinking his boss would find the comment funny.

"Paul, I just called your office, and they told me that they haven't seen you there in two days," Mr. Brownlee said. His voice was calm but determined. "Now I understand why."

"Bah, they don't care. And I don't care."

"I do care. Paul, you're fired."

Mr. Brownlee hung up the call. Paul sat there and stared at the phone for a long time. Then the alcohol and fatigue won, and he fell asleep, dropping the phone on the floor. What was left of the beer spilled on his clothes and the couch. Soon, his snoring filled the room.

When Paul woke up four hours later, his bladder was about to burst. Holding his pee, he navigated to the bathroom and got his zipper open at a very last moment. What a big relief! Listening to the gurgling sound, he looked at himself in the mirror. Paul wasn't a particularly handsome man, but the face that was looking back from the mirror shocked him.

My wife's dying. I banished Alex from his home. And I lost my job, he thought and regretted what he had done. *If Tommy were here, he would at least send me to the hospital to see my wife.*

Thomas Hanson wasn't there, and Paul didn't feel comfortable meeting his old friend just a few days after he had fired Tommy's wife. Still, he decided that tomorrow he would go to the hospital to see Sara. She might not have many days, but he decided to spend them with her.

There was a heavy rain. Sara Wesley could hear it even though she couldn't see the window that was behind the curtain. She was lying on a hospital bed at Fairmont Memorial. Her hands were crossed, and she was talking to God.

Sara no longer prayed that the doctors would find a way to operate on the tumor. Neither did she wish for more weeks or months. If her remaining time would be painless, and if God would take her to Heaven, that was all she could hope for.

"I have lived faithfully and followed your will, Father," she whispered, and a peaceful silence filled her mind.

There was a knock on the door, and a young nurse stepped in, bringing her lunch. Sara rose to sit on the bed. The nurse set the tray in front of her and gave her a sympathetic smile. Despite his young age, Sara wasn't his first hospice patient. He had seen many people dying in the hospital. Most of them were older than Sara.

"Thank you, young man. That soup was perfect," Sara said when the nurse returned to the room twenty minutes later.

"You're welcome, Mrs. Wesley," the nurse said and was about to collect the dishes.

"You are very sexy, young man. Would you mind joining me in the bed?" Sara asked, touching the nurse's hand.

"Just a minute, ma'am," the nurse said, and pressed the button on the wall.

He looked at the bowl on the tray and noticed that Sara had eaten only half of the soup. It didn't surprise him. Many patients lost their appetites. Either it was too hurtful to swallow, or they just didn't remember that they were hungry.

Sara moved in her bed and seemed a bit anxious. Then she started to unbutton her shirt. Luckily, the doctor on call came quickly. Apparently, the morning had been silent.

"You called me, Harry?" the doctor asked.

"Yup. Mrs. Wesley is suffering from some personality changes. She wanted to have sex with me," he said.

"Aha, let's see what we can do," the doctor said. "Can't blame her, though. You're quite handsome," she added.

The nurse blushed lightly and smiled at the doctor, who could have been his mother. Then he collected all the dishes and left the room. Sara was obviously disappointed that the woman in a white coat had come to the room and interrupted them.

"Mrs. Wesley, let's put you back to a lying position," the doctor said as she helped Sara to lie down.

"Ow, my head hurts," Sara said, and felt like an elephant had just sat on her forehead. Then she lost vision in her right eye.

"I'll give you some medication for the pain," the doctor said, taking a syringe from a locked cabin on the other side of the room.

Without saying a word, she pulled the needle through the plastic cork and injected the medicine into the tube that led to the cannula, which was attached to Sara's hand. Monitoring Sara's reactions, she waited fifteen seconds, watching her watch. The dose was enough to take the pain away, but it was only a matter of time until she would need a more effective drug.

"I can't see with my right eye," Sara said.

"How long has it been like that?" the doctor asked.

"It went black only now."

"The tumor is causing pressure in your brain. I can't promise that you will get your vision back in that eye."

The doctor checked both of Sara's eyes but, as expected, couldn't find anything abnormal there. The problem was in her brain, and it was worrying that her condition was deteriorating that quickly.

"I don't have many days, do I?" Sara asked, as if she had been reading the doctor's face.

"The X-ray shows that you have a few cancer cells circulating in your brain fluid," the doctor said. "If and when you develop more, they will start blocking the flow of the fluid, and that will be severe."

"How long?" Sara asked again.

"It's impossible to predict. It can be anything from two weeks to three months," the doctor said, looking her patient in the eyes. Sara looked back with the only eye that was functioning.

Sara realized that she might not be spending Thanksgiving with her family. Even though she was prepared to leave, she would have wanted to spend one more evening with them. One more time when all of them would sit around the dining room table so that she could say farewell to her husband and son.

She had been thinking about her last encounter with Alex the whole morning. The idea that Alex could be gay was terrifying because, if it was true, it meant that they would not meet again in Heaven. She would do anything not to lose her son to the devil, but still she regretted that she had tried to separate Alex from his friend.

I don't want to die before I have talked to Alex, she thought, and a tear rolled down her cheek.

The doctor left the room, and half an hour later, Alex was standing at the door and looking at his mother. Sara couldn't remember if she had ever seen, even when she \ still had vision in both her eyes, Alex having such a scared face.

"Mom, how are you?" Alex asked and approached her slowly.

"I'm okay, honey. It's just the medicine that makes me look awful," she said smiling and was grateful that God had sent her son to visit her in the hospital.

"Dad called me," Alex said hesitantly. "He said that … um, that it's severe."

Sara realized that Alex wanted to know how long she would live but couldn't find the courage to ask. Sara thought about what she would say. It annoyed her that everybody who visited her in the room was so desperate to pity her, like it would help her to heal. She was dying, that was a fact, but she wanted to do it with dignity.

"They give me good medicine here. I don't feel any pain," she lied.

"That's good to hear," Alex said as he sat in the chair that was by the bed.

"But you're right. The tumor is aggressive, and they can't remove it." She paused, and her voice cracked as she added, "I might not have many weeks."

She looked at Alex, whose eyes shone with tears. Her son had suddenly grown up and become a handsome young man. She hadn't realized it when she and Paul had visited Eastwood University just a few days ago, but now that they were alone in the hospital room, it was so evident.

"Don't cry, darling. I've made peace with God."

"I'm gonna miss you," Alex said and swallowed.

"I'm going to miss you, too."

Sara felt how Alex took hold of her hand. It was the first time she'd felt a connection with him in such a long time. Maybe God was giving her a sign that now was the proper moment to talk to him.

"Let's talk about something happier," she said. "Are there any pretty girls at Eastwood?"

"Huh? Sure. There are plenty of girls on campus," Alex answered.

"Are you dating anyone?" she asked, hoping that this would be an easy discussion.

She saw Alex blushing a bit and thought that it was a good sign. Her son was apparently dating someone and was just a bit shy to admit it to her. Patiently, she waited to hear what Alex would say.

"No, Mom. I've made friends with some girls in my classes, but I'm not dating any of them," Alex said.

That was a disappointment. On the other hand, Alex had been in Eddington less than two months. He would still have time. Suddenly, Sara realized that she wouldn't see when Alex graduated. The thought was too depressing, and she forced it away from her mind.

"It would just make me happy to know that you have found someone," she said.

Alex nodded, and Sara felt how he squeezed her hand gently. She wanted to ask about Liam. There were too many questions, and some of them were too scary to be said aloud. *Maybe I could ask if Liam is dating someone*, she thought and felt aching pain at her temples.

She closed her eyes, even the one that couldn't see anything. For a moment, she heard only the clock ticking on the wall and the humming sound coming from the air conditioning. Then the pain was gone, and she opened her eyes again. The white walls and the blue curtain were still there. And so was her son, sitting next to her.

"Are there any pretty girls on campus?" she asked, turning to face Alex.

"Um ... Mom, you just asked that," Alex said, and her expression became worried.

"Did I?" she said, confused.

The doctor had told her that the tumor might impact her mood or memory, but she was pretty sure that she hadn't asked that question. But why would her son be lying? And why couldn't she remember anything they had been discussing?

"Mom, are you okay? Should I call a doctor?" Alex said, looking more and more worried.

"No," she snapped. "I'm fine."

"Okay, sorry," Alex said and let go of her hand.

"Alex, there's something I need to know, and this is important," she said and stared at him with her only functioning eye.

"Yes, what is it?"

"Do you follow the will of God?"

She saw how Alex stood up and looked around the room. Then he found a button on the wall and pressed it. Sara couldn't understand how the button would help Alex to answer her question. She had to know the answer.

"Do you follow the will of God?" she asked again.

She repeated the question, and every time it felt more and more painful. It was like God was attempting to give her the answer. She tried harder, and the pain became more and more intense. Then, suddenly, she didn't feel anything.

Chapter 8

Alex looked at the blueberry pie that was on the plate in front of him. It looked delicious, just like everything else Liam's mother cooked in her kitchen. The morning after his father had called, he and Liam had driven to Fairmont.

"How's your mother?" Liam asked.

Alex had hardly said a word since he had returned to Liam's house from the hospital. They had gathered around the kitchen table with Liam's parents, Jenny and Matt Green, who were shocked by the news.

"I don't know," Alex said, looking at the others. "First, she was okay, I guess. Then, suddenly, she lost her memory and started to talk about God and blacked out," he said.

"Oh dear," Mrs. Green said and instinctively raised her hand in front of her mouth.

"Is she…?" Liam said but couldn't finish the sentence.

"The doctor gave her some medicine. She's still alive but tired and not feeling very well," Alex said. He was struggling to hold back his tears.

Liam rose and hugged his boyfriend, who rested his head against Liam's chest and began to cry. Liam's parents sat there quietly, and his mother's eyes became moist. They had never met Alex's parents, but seeing Alex so miserable was bad enough.

"Alex, you don't have to talk about it if you don't want to. Just remember that we all will support you," Mrs. Green said. "Just let us know if there's anything we can do for you."

"Thanks," Alex said and gave her a small smile.

Alex liked Liam's parents. They were such good people. Sometimes, he felt a bit jealous of Liam because his own parents were not as nice, especially when it came to his relationship with Liam. His parents would never accept it like Liam's parents had done.

There was another thing that was bothering Alex. During the argument about their living arrangements, he had said something to Liam that he now regretted. He was sure that Liam remembered those words, but he was just too kind not to remind him.

I fucking hate my parents. I wish they were dead. That was what he had said. Naturally, he understood that his mother getting sick wasn't his fault, but somehow he couldn't stop thinking that he had gotten what he wanted.

"Is it okay if I sleep here?" Alex asked. "I can sleep on the sofa."

"Of course, you can," Mrs. Green said, "but not on the sofa. Liam's bed is big enough for both of you."

As she stood up, Alex looked at Liam's father, worried that Mr. Green wouldn't approve of Liam sleeping in the same bed with Alex. Liam's father was concerned, but not for the reason that Alex had first believed.

"How's your dad? He wasn't at the hospital?" Mr. Green asked.

Alex shook his head. The event at his home returned to his mind. *He hadn't even wanted to see Mom*, Alex thought.

"He was drunk when I went there," Alex said.

"I'm really sorry to hear that," Mr. Green said and nodded at Liam, who wrapped his arms around Alex again.

"I had to leave. I think he was trying to hit me or something," Alex said. His voice was hardly louder than a whisper.

Liam's father stood up from his seat and patted Alex on the shoulder. Then he walked to the window. For a while, he just watched the birds in the garden, and it seemed that he was thinking something.

"My parents died in a car accident soon after Liam was born," Mr. Green said. "I'm not saying that I know how you feel, and you are even younger than I was then."

Alex looked at Mr. Green and gave him a weak smile. Then he did something unexpected; he stood up and hugged Liam's father. At that moment, Mr. Green felt more like a father to him than his own father, who was probably very drunk right then, if not passed out already.

"Alex is going through a rough time," Mr. Green told his son. "I want you to support him in all possible ways."

Liam nodded and looked at Alex, who was grateful that he had his boyfriend. Alex didn't even want to think about the alternative. Without Liam, he would have had to go through all this alone now that his father didn't seem to be able to support him.

Once they had finished eating, the four of them sat in the living room watching a movie on TV. For Alex, it was as good a distraction as he could get, but his mother and father were constantly on his mind.

At first, Alex had felt a bit uncomfortable when Liam had sat on his lap on the sofa while Liam's parents were in the same room. As neither of his parents showed the slightest hint of disapproval, Alex wrapped his arms around his boyfriend and enjoyed the closeness.

When the movie ended, everyone felt tired, and the boys went to Liam's bedroom where his mother had made the bed. A smile rose on Alex's face when he saw how she had arranged the pillows next to each other, with only one big blanket that they would share.

My mother would never make us such a bed, Alex thought. That brought to his mind the fact that Sara Wesley would most likely never make them any kind of bed.

She would die without knowing how special Liam was to her son.

"I'm sorry that I can't take you with me to the hospital," Alex said to Liam.

"Don't worry. I understand," Liam said softly.

"But your parents are so kind to me," Alex began to say.

"Shh," Liam said and moved closer to Alex.

He stripped Alex's shirt and was rewarded with a view of his muscular chest. He touched Alex's pecs, and they both felt the electricity between them. Alex knew how much Liam loved to take off his clothes, so he stood still and let his boyfriend unbuckle his belt and unbutton his jeans.

"Mmm…," Liam murmured when Alex was standing there in only his boxers. "I see someone likes me," he said and rubbed Alex's crotch.

"We both like you very much," Alex said, kissing his boyfriend.

Liam checked that the door was locked, and soon they were naked under the big blanket, kissing and hugging each other. It had been a rough day for Alex, and he wanted to get as close to his boyfriend as possible. Liam's hands roaming his back made him horny.

"I can't believe we are doing this when your parents are oblivious on the other side of the wall," Alex whispered.

"Oblivious?" Liam said. "You really think they can't guess what we are doing here?" He flashed a wide grin.

"Let's not talk about your parents. Or mine."

"Agreed."

Alex woke up the following morning and felt Liam's arm around him. Liam was already awake, and as soon as he noticed Alex's eyes opening, he planted a kiss on Alex's lips.

"Good morning, my sexy swimmer," Liam whispered.

Alex smiled and felt how Liam's hand was moving downward along his belly. Soon, it found its target.

"Uh ... I need to pee," Alex said.

"Mmm ... are you absolutely sure?" Liam said.

"You're evil," Alex laughed, "but I really need to go."

Liam watched as Alex got dressed. Even with his bed hair, Alex looked gorgeous. The jock was lean, and his muscles were well defined but not too big. Liam could still remember the autumn day two years ago when he had first seen Alex. A lot had happened in their lives since then, but he was happy that they had just slept together in the same bed in his parents' house. It was so much more than he could have ever imagined.

When Alex came back, his face had become serious. Liam knew immediately that his boyfriend was thinking something, and he knew to wait until Alex was ready to talk to him. It didn't take long.

"I've been thinking," Alex said.

Liam had a bunch of sarcastic comments in his mind, but he decided that now was not the time for those.

"Mom might die any day," Alex said matter-of-factly. "Should I come out to her before it's too late?"

"Oh … I didn't expect that," Liam said.

Alex sat on the edge of the bed, and Liam moved next to him and wrapped them in the blanket. The house was silent, and Alex could hear the raindrops beating a gentle tattoo on the roof as he tried to find the words to explain his feelings to Liam.

"I don't want Mom to die without knowing the real me," Alex said.

"Your mom knows the real you," Liam said. "Whether you like girls or boys doesn't change that."

Liam's words made sense, but Alex knew that his mother wouldn't see it the same way. He was sure that she would see him like an entirely different person, and now Alex wasn't sure whether she deserved to know the truth or to be kept in the dark. Either way, he had only once chance and little time to make the decision.

"I would also like to let her know that I'm happy," Alex said.

"Seems that you've been thinking about this a lot," Liam said.

"I hardly slept last night."

They heard the front door open, and soon there was a knock on Liam's door. Then Liam's father opened the door and stepped in, keeping his hand in front of his eyes.

"Are you decent?" he asked.

"Ha-ha," Liam said and blushed.

Mr. Green lowered his hand and looked at the boys. He was happy to notice that both of them seemed to be in a good mood. At least both of them were smiling. They had just started college, and Mr. Green was sorry that Alex had to go through all this right now. He should be at college, enjoying his life while he was still young.

"We woke up a bit earlier and went for a walk in the park," Liam's father said. "Jenny is preparing breakfast. It should be ready soon."

"Thanks," both boys said almost simultaneously.

After Mr. Green had left, Liam wrapped his arms around Alex and hugged him. He wanted to comfort his boyfriend who would lose his mother far too soon. They sat on the bed and held each other for a long time.

"I love you so much," Alex said with his voice cracking as he looked at Liam with his teary eyes. He couldn't stop thinking his mother and how little time she might have.

Liam tightened the grip of his arms, squeezing the jock like a big teddy bear. "I love you, too," he said. After a short pause, he added, "You're not alone," and let Alex cry against his chest.

Once he had calmed down, Alex went to the bathroom to take a quick shower before breakfast. He was taken by surprise when Liam joined him under the showerhead a couple of minutes later. It was less of a surprise that Liam took the opportunity to rub soap on his body very thoroughly.

Mr. Green couldn't help smiling when he caught the boys red-handed coming from the bathroom together. They had assumed that he was still in the kitchen with his wife. To Liam's relief, he didn't say a word but continued reading the newspaper. Alex blushed and followed his boyfriend to his bedroom, avoiding eye contact with Liam's father.

"Have you decided if you're going to tell your mom?" Liam asked when they were putting their clothes on in Liam's room.

"I can't make up my mind," Alex said, frustrated. "What do you think? Should I?"

"I wouldn't," Liam said honestly. "Of course, it's your decision, but I'm worried that she won't take it well."

"Maybe you're right."

An hour later, Alex parked his Mustang in the parking lot in front of Fairmont Memorial Hospital. He was alone. It would have been nice to go there with Liam, and Alex was painfully aware that, if Liam's mother were sick, they would go to visit her as a couple.

Why did I get the worst parents in the world? Alex swore and looked up at the sky, where he thought God was. As soon as he entered the palliative care department on the third floor, he regretted his thoughts. The smell of death was hovering in the corridors. It was too concrete a reminder of why he was there.

Alex stood for a while in front of the door before he found the courage to push the door open and step in. His face was relieved, and all the tension faded away from his body when he saw his mother. She was still alive.

"Hi, Alex," she said, almost too cheerfully.

"Hi … um, how are you?" Alex asked.

"They just pumped me full of medicine," she said.

"Okay, cool, I guess," Alex said and realized that he didn't have flowers or chocolate with him. Weren't those things that people gave to patients while visiting them in hospitals?

His mother seemed to be in a much better mood than when Alex had visited her the day before. She was smiling and even lively considering that she was lying on the bed. There was a cannula in her right hand. They used it to nourish her as the doctor had recommended that she not raise her head from the pillow. Too much movement could increase the pressure of the brain fluid.

"Alex, I'm sorry that I tried to make you move," she said.

"That's okay. I just want to live on campus like everyone else," Alex said, wondering why she had changed her mind.

"I thought that your own apartment would have given you a more peaceful environment to study," she said. "It was silly." She gave a quiet laugh.

"It's not silly, and I appreciate your support."

Alex hugged her carefully. How ironic it was that both of them were lying, but it made them feel better. Maybe it was the growing awareness of the sand trickling down in her hourglass that brought false politeness to their discussion.

"How are your studies progressing?" she asked.

"Very well," Alex said.

He didn't want to worry her with the detail that he might not pass general chemistry and might need to take the course again next year. It was better to let his mother, who paid his tuition, believe that he was doing well, which he was in many subjects.

"How's Liam?" Mrs. Wesley asked.

"He's okay. Excited about the history program," Alex said, surprised that she mentioned him.

"Is he in Fairmont, too?" she asked.

"Yes. We drove here together. Liam wanted to see his parents."

"How thoughtful of him."

He hadn't mentioned to his mother that he had spent the previous night at the Greens' house. Alex's father had been too drunk for Alex to want to spend time at home. Besides, he had enjoyed sleeping with Liam in the bed that Liam's mother had made for them.

Alex walked by the window and looked at the parking lot. He saw his red car under a big tree and thought about how nice it would be to jump into the car and drive away. He and his mother were having this superficial discussion, where both of them said what they expected the other to want to hear. It frustrated him.

After glancing at his car one more time, Alex returned to sit beside his mother's bed. What he didn't notice was that his father's black Audi was parked on the other side of the parking lot.

"Alex, I don't have much time," Mrs. Wesley said. "I just want to know that everything is good, and you're happy."

"I'm happy, Mom," Alex said.

It was already the third time they'd had this same discussion, and it still made both of their eyes moist.

"Promise me that you will make me beautiful grandchildren," she said as a teardrop ran down her cheek.

"I can't promise you that," Alex said, and his heart started to beat faster.

"I'll see them from Heaven."

"I didn't mean that."

It was like time had stopped, and Alex could feel his pulse. He was sweating, and his chest felt hot, like someone was burning a bonfire under his seat. They looked at each other, and both of them knew what he was about to say next.

"Mom, I'm gay," Alex said, feeling faint.

He had done it. He had told his mother something he had feared saying aloud for the last two years. For two years of his life, he had been hiding it, and now he was there in front of his dying mother, and his whole body was shaking.

Alex's father, who had been standing at the door, left before Alex or his mother could notice him. He nearly ran down the stairs and left the hospital without saying a word to anybody. His car had already disappeared when Alex fled the building crying a few moments later.

Chapter 9

It was a cold Saturday afternoon in November, just before Thanksgiving Day. Paul Wesley couldn't find any reason to celebrate. He had lost his job and had not been able to find a new one. Even the fact that he had mostly stopped drinking hadn't helped.

"Here's the key to your apartment," the landlord said.

Paul looked at the man in shabby clothes and took the key from his hand. After losing his job, Paul had been forced to sell the house since he no longer had money to pay the mortgage. An unemployed widower with a drinking problem wasn't the best customer for the bank. It was miracle enough that he had been able to find a rental apartment.

"Call me if you need anything," the landlord said and began to walk away. "December's rent is due by next Wednesday," he shouted on his way.

"Sure," Paul muttered and opened the door to the apartment.

The apartment was furnished, not that the furniture from the Wesleys' big house would fit there. The floor of the only room was covered in dust. On the left, there was a small kitchen corner and behind that a bathroom. On the right, Paul saw an alcove where he was supposed to sleep from now on.

Letting out a heavy sigh, Paul carried the first moving box to the small table, which was accompanied by two chairs. That would be his new dining space. Soon, Thomas Hanson stepped in with another box and put it on the floor next to the table.

"Thanks for your help, Tommy," Paul said.

"No problem," Thomas replied.

Both of them knew that Paul meant a lot more than just carrying a box or helping in the move. And it was equally self-evident that he would not have the vocabulary to elaborate his gratitude further. Those two college friends didn't talk about feelings. It wasn't their thing.

After Thomas had heard that Sara had been taken to the hospital, he had appeared at Paul's front door. Paul had been so wasted that he had hardly realized that Thomas had entered the kitchen and poured all his booze in the sink. The next two days, Paul had slept on the Hansons' sofa, which wasn't the same one he had used for the same purpose eighteen years earlier.

It had been Thomas who had helped Paul to sell his house. Needless to say, Thomas had organized most of the practicalities when Sara had died three weeks later. Paul had wanted just a small funeral, and his friend had honored his wishes.

"I'll pick you up tomorrow, and then we'll drive together to the church," Thomas said after they had carried all the moving boxes to Paul's apartment.

"Thanks. I'll try to find my black suit in one of the boxes," Paul said.

Thomas nodded to his friend and hesitated a bit. "Um … you said Alex won't be coming to the funeral. Should I try to talk to him one more time?" he asked then.

"No," Paul said quickly. "Um … he doesn't want to see Sara or me," he added before realizing again that Sara wasn't alive anymore.

Thomas didn't ask for the reason. He noticed that the topic was difficult for Paul. Something must have happened to put the boy on bad terms with his parents. Thomas, or Coach Hanson, had been Alex's swimming coach at Fairmont High School, and he remembered Alex having some problems with his teammates. Thomas didn't know the details, and he had never talked about that with Paul.

"Whatever it is, I hope you get it sorted out," Thomas said, wondering what kind of a son would not want to come to his mother's funeral. He would have wanted to speak to Alex, but out of respect for Paul, he decided to stay away.

Paul nodded and gave his friend a forced smile.

After Thomas had left, Paul started to open the boxes and put things in their places. He realized that, if Sara were still alive, she would have vacuumed the room first. Paul didn't bother. He had lost everything: his job, his house, his wife, and his son.

The only people Paul had left in his life were Thomas and Alma, and they were the only guests at Sara's funeral the following morning. Paul assumed that Sara's relatives would be pissed off when they realized that they had not been invited, but Paul didn't care.

On Monday morning, Paul sat on the porch of his new apartment. Sara's memorial service had been small-scale, just like he had desired. They had been married for twenty years, and now it was over. For the first time in his life, Paul felt lonely.

As he didn't have anything better to do, he looked back on his life and what he had accomplished. He had majored in sales and marketing and had spent most of his career working for Henderson Watson Sport. He hadn't told Sara that Mr. Brownlee had fired him.

The end of his employment was too embarrassing, and Paul forced his thoughts to those days fifteen years ago when Alex had been a toddler. He had been playing in their backyard with the three-year-old kid, who loved to kick the soccer ball with him. It made Paul smile until he remembered the words that he had heard in the hospital.

Mom, I'm gay.

However hard he tried not to think of them, those were the words that Paul would remember the rest of his life. No son could humiliate his father worse than Alex had done. That was the moment when Paul Wesley realized he didn't have a son anymore.

Paul regretted that they hadn't had more children. Both Sara and he had been too career-oriented, and they had felt that one was enough, especially as it was a boy. Now it was too late.

It's that fucking perv Alex started to hang out with. He turned my son into a fag, Paul figured. He would have visited Liam's parents and told them a couple of truths about their son if he only knew where they lived. Maybe it was better that he didn't.

Wallowing in self-pity, Paul went to get a beer from the fridge. He had promised Thomas he would stay sober, but he thought that, if he had only one, he wouldn't break the promise. Then he took another and a third one.

There was one thing Paul couldn't understand. He was very sure that he had heard what Alex said in the hospital. There was no second-guessing that. *But why didn't Sara ever say anything to me?* Paul kept wondering. Sara had died only some weeks after that fateful morning when Paul lost his only son, and he had visited Sara several times in the hospital.

She was ill and weak, but she couldn't have approved of the decision Alex had made, Paul thought. They had been married for twenty years, and he knew his wife. Sara had been a well-educated woman, who had high morals and pure values. *Maybe Alex is rebelling against us*, Paul realized, remembering how he had challenged his father's old-fashioned opinions sometimes.

Whatever the reason for Alex's reckless behavior, Paul didn't want to have anything to do with him anymore. The boy was now on his own. Luckily, he had remembered to put an end to the automatic transfers from Sara's and his bank account to Alex. If the boy wanted to fuck around, he wouldn't do it with Paul's money.

Feeling frustrated and angry, Paul went to the fridge, only to learn that there was no more beer left. He slammed the door with such force that it bounced open. Kicking the fridge with his foot and leaning his body against the door, he finally got it closed. Then Paul put on his jacket and walked out. There was a bar around the corner.

When Paul tried to enter the small pub in a red brick building, he found that it was closed and wouldn't open for many hours. It wasn't even midday yet, and the customers would still be at work. At least those who had jobs. Piqued, Paul looked around and saw an old man standing on the corner of the building.

"Wanna buy some whiskey? Fifty bucks," the man said and showed the bottle to Paul.

"Mind your own fucking business," Paul grumbled and turned around to leave, but realized that the old man was his best chance.

"Okay, sorry, tough day," he said and approached the man.

"This will help," the man said as he looked at Paul.

The old man knew his clients. There were plenty in the neighborhood, and he had been sure that Paul would buy the bottle. A drunk needs his fuel, and cheap scotch with a ridiculous margin was a great business that any honest businessman would envy. Besides, his sales article was tax-free.

Paul returned to his apartment and took a glass from the cupboard. He poured the whiskey until the glass was half full and then sat on the sofa. The magical elixir burned his throat and healed his soul, and it also made him return to the old man the following day, and the day after.

Chapter 10

Frustrated, Alex put the phone back in his pocket. He had tried to reach his mother for several days already, but she hadn't answered. What was alarming was that the recorded message was now telling him that the number was not in use. Puzzled, Alex looked at his boyfriend, as if Liam would know the answer.

"You think she might have … died?" Liam said, concerned.

"Yes … no … I don't know," Alex said. "It doesn't make any sense."

If her phone was cut off, that meant that she had died several days ago. In that case, his father would have called him already. Alex couldn't think of any other explanation than that they had terminated her mobile plan because they thought she wouldn't need the phone anymore.

"I should have paid my tuition already," Alex agonized. For some reason, he hadn't received the money from his parents this month.

"I can loan you money," Liam offered.

"Thanks, I think I have no other option," Alex said, embarrassed.

Liam stood up and kissed his boyfriend. Then they hugged, which led to groping each other. Soon they were in bed, and Alex pulled down Liam's college pants and boxers.

"If this is the way you pay back, I should loan you money more often," Liam smirked.

"Nah. This is just the interest. You'll get your money back as soon as my parents transfer more to my account," Alex said.

They kept making out until Alex's phone started to ring. Quickly, he pulled up his pants and took the phone from his pocket. Alex didn't recognize the number, which was a disappointment as he had expected either of his parents to call.

The call was from the office of Dean Curtis. The secretary told Alex that the Dean would like to meet him as soon as possible. He tried to ask why, but the secretary just recommended that he hurry. That was odd.

"Dean Curtis? What does she want?" Liam asked after Alex had ended the call.

"They just said she wants to meet me," Alex said, confused.

Alex took clean jeans and a dress shirt from the closet. He had never met Dean Curtis personally, and whatever she wanted to talk to him about, he wanted to at least have proper clothes for the meeting. Then he left the dorm room and walked across the yard to the main building where her office was.

It was already six o'clock in the evening only a couple of days before Thanksgiving. They would have some classes the following morning, and then everything at the university would stop for the weekend. It was strange that the Dean was working this late.

The administration wing was as silent as Alex had expected. He walked directly to the secretary's room and asked to see Dean Curtis. She opened the door to the Dean's office and asked Alex to enter.

"Mr. Wesley," Dean Curtis said as she stood up to shake hands with Alex. Then she gestured for Alex to sit in the chair on the other side of her big desk.

"I got your application some weeks ago, and I was about to approve it," Dean Curtis said.

"Oh," Alex said, intimidated by the severe expression on the Dean's face. He had no clue which application she was referring to but didn't have time to ask before she continued.

"Then I got a very unpleasant phone call this morning," she said.

"Um ... I'm not sure if I follow you," Alex said.

"This university does not tolerate discrimination of any kind," she said, raising her voice a bit and staring at Alex, who was more and more confused.

He hadn't sent the Dean any application. The chemistry professor had given him an F, which meant that Alex had to take the course again next year. And his studies in signal processing were not progressing well, but it seemed that the Dean wasn't referring to any of these.

"I'm sorry, but I don't understand what you are referring to," Alex said and realized that he was holding his breath.

"Your roommate is gay, right?" the Dean said.

"Um, yes, he is," Alex said, feeling totally confused.

"And you want to move to live off-campus because of that," the Dean said, her entire demeanor reflecting annoyance.

Suddenly everything became clear to Alex. His mother had to have something to do with this. Alex had come out to her, and now she was trying to separate him and Liam. Alex couldn't think of any other explanation.

"No, ma'am. I would like you to reject the application," Alex said in a panic that he might have to move from the dorm room.

"Mr. Wesley, you can be sure that I'll reject it," the Dean said, and her voice was still angry. "And I'm seriously considering suspending you for the rest of the semester."

"No, you don't understand," Alex said. "I didn't send in the application."

"If it wasn't you, who was it?"

"My mother must have sent it. Liam, my roommate, is my boyfriend, and she doesn't want us to live in the same room."

The Dean looked at Alex for a long time. The expression on her face, which had been angry, became more and more sympathetic. Then she took the application paper from the desk and ripped it, which brought a smile to Alex's face.

"Mr. Wesley, I'm glad we got this sorted out," she said, and her voice was now warm and friendly.

"I'm sorry about what my mother did," Alex said and stood up to leave the office.

"Don't be. It's not your fault," the Dean said, "and just let me know if you need any help."

Feeling relieved, Alex began walking back to the dorm. One more time, he tried to call to his mother but was greeted again by the recording that the number was not in use. He was about to call his father when he saw Scott hurrying toward him.

"Hi, Scott," Alex greeted his friend.

"Um … hi," Scott said, and Alex could recognize from his voice that something was wrong.

"Are you okay?" Alex asked hesitantly.

"My brother was in a fight. He's in the hospital," Scott said. "Actually, I'm a bit busy. I just heard about it, and I'm leaving for home."

"Shit. Okay, let's talk later," Alex said and followed Scott with his gaze as he was running toward the bus stop carrying a big bag.

Scott's brother, Shawn, was in high school, and Scott had worried that some kids bullied him because Shawn was more feminine than the other high school boys. Suddenly, Alex remembered how he had teased Liam with Rick and Sam.

It was embarrassing and felt childish now, but Alex had believed that making fun of Liam would make his growing feelings toward other high school boys fade away. It hadn't, luckily, and now he and Liam were happily together. Alex hoped that everything would turn out well for Shawn, too.

Jenny and Matt Green looked at each other, confused, and neither of them knew what to say. It was the night before Thanksgiving, and Alex and Liam had just arrived in Fairmont.

"You mean that Mom is dead?" Alex asked. He wasn't sure, but it felt like Liam's mother had just expressed her condolences.

"You didn't know?" Mr. Green asked.

"Fuck. No," Alex cursed and apologized as soon as he understood what he had said.

Liam's mother had heard the news that morning when she had visited the mall to get some groceries for the weekend. She had been surprised that Liam hadn't told her anything when they had called the previous day. Now, she was even more surprised that, apparently, Alex didn't even know that his mother had died, and he had not been at the funeral last Sunday.

"I need to go home," Alex said, putting down the bags he was carrying.

"You want me to join you?" Liam asked.

"Um … maybe it's better if I go alone," Alex said.

"When will you come back?"

"I don't know."

The boys had planned to stay at Liam's house over Thanksgiving weekend. Of course, Alex would have visited his mother at the hospital, hoping to see his father there, too, even though both of them had been ignoring his calls. Now he knew why his mother hadn't answered his calls.

Liam watched, worried, as his boyfriend rushed to his red Mustang and left with such speed that the back tires almost left a black mark on the road. *I shouldn't have let him go alone in such a shocked state of mind*, Liam thought and wished that Alex would at least call him soon.

Alex parked his car in front of the house. His father's car had to be in the garage as he couldn't see it anywhere. On the other side of the driveway, there was a red SUV, which Alex had not seen before.

Wondering whether his father would be at home, Alex walked to the front door. He was about to ring the bell, but then took his key and opened the door. He shouted for his father, and soon a scared woman appeared in the hall. She was carrying a small baby on her hip.

"Who are you, and how did you get in?" she asked.

"Huh? I'm Alex, and … I live here," Alex said. "Or, actually, my father lives here," he corrected.

"Jeffrey, come here!" the woman shouted to someone, apparently to her husband.

"What's going on?" Jeffrey asked.

"He came here with his own keys and says his father lives here," she said, pointing at Alex.

Alex and the man, Jeffrey, looked at each other for a moment. Alex felt like he had fallen into some alternate reality where his mother was dead and some strange people lived in their house. Luckily, Jeffrey seemed to understand what had happened.

"Your father is Paul Wesley?" Jeffrey asked.

"Yes, he is," Alex said.

"We bought this house from your father a month ago, and we moved here last weekend," Jeffrey said.

"Oh, I'm sorry. I didn't know," Alex said as he took a couple of steps back. "Do you know where my father moved?" he asked hopefully.

The couple looked at each other, and both of them shook their heads. Alex apologized one more time and gave his key to the man. Then he left his old home, most likely for the last time in his life, and walked back to his car.

Where is all my stuff that I left at home? Alex realized that he had taken only part of his belongings with him to Eddington. They didn't have too much space in their dorm room. For a short time, Alex considered returning to the house but realized then that his stuff would no longer be there.

Alex tried to call his father, but he didn't answer. Frustrated, he sent a text message asking for his father's new address and started the engine of his Mustang to drive back to Liam's house. Halfway there, his phone beeped, and Alex stopped to read the message. It explained everything but was something he wouldn't have ever wanted to receive.

I know you're a FAG. Stop calling me. You are no longer my son.

Alex sat in the car, and his hand that was holding the phone began to shake when he read the message for the third time. The words hurt him worse than anything in his life. He refused to cry since he felt that his father wasn't worth the tears, but he wanted to calm down before facing Liam and his parents.

Alex parked his car near the park where his high school swim team used to organize parties. It was dark, and only the street lights illuminated the area that brought back so many memories. He even saw the stone where he and Sofia had been sitting when they had kissed the first time.

Alex had dated two girls, Sofia and Sarah, in high school. Both of them had been mistakes. It had been the time when Alex wasn't yet ready to accept who he was. And now that he could finally admit that he was gay, even hold his boyfriend's hand on the university campus, his mother had died and his father had turned him down.

How did he know? Alex suddenly realized that he had told only his mother. He remembered her reaction when Alex finally got the words out of his mouth. She had been shocked and asked Alex to leave the room. Two days later, she had called and told Alex that it was between him and God, and he should never tell his father.

I didn't say a word to Dad, but who did? Alex asked himself but could not find the answer. They had talked briefly one more time, and it was the last time Alex had heard his mother's voice. Neither of them had mentioned his sexual orientation, and they had just chatted about how they would spend Christmas together. Most likely, both of them had known that she wouldn't live that long.

Alex sat on the stone where he and Sofia had shared their first kiss, wishing that it had happened with Liam. *Fuck, I'm an orphan*, Alex thought, and now he couldn't hold back tears. There had been growing tension between him and his parents, and especially his last two years in high school had been difficult. It was far too late to fix things with his mother, and Alex wasn't positive that his father would ever accept him.

I should call Liam, Alex thought and took out his phone to inform his boyfriend that he would be there soon. Unfortunately, the battery was dead. Just when he thought that things couldn't get any worse, he saw a familiar car stopping. Alex tensed when he realized who emerged from the car.

"Well, well. Has the faggot come home? Your parents must be proud of you."

It was Rick Donovan, Alex's former best friend, and despite the darkness, Alex could see the cocky smirk on his face.

Liam was sick with worry. Alex had left the previous night, and he hadn't come back yet. Liam had tried to call him several times, but it always went to his voice mail. *What has happened to him?* Liam wondered, turning his spoon in the cereal bowl.

"I just put the turkey in the oven. Do you think Alex will have dinner with us?" Liam's mother shouted from the kitchen.

"No idea," Liam said and stared at his phone. It didn't start ringing.

"You haven't heard anything from him?" Liam's father asked. He had finished his breakfast and was reading the newspaper in the dining room.

"No," Liam sighed. "Can I borrow your car?"

His father nodded.

Liam left the half-eaten bowl of cereal on the table and took the car keys from the drawer in the hallway. Then he hurried to his father's Nissan Maxima and started the engine. Liam wasn't used to driving a car, but he made it to Alex's house. The disappointment was written on his face when the red Mustang wasn't there.

Next Liam drove to the hospital, only to find that Alex's car wasn't there either. *Where could he have gone?* Liam pondered. He drove aimlessly around Fairmont almost an hour but didn't see a glimpse of his boyfriend. Liam parked the car near the mall and stepped out.

It was Thanksgiving morning, and the mall was closed. Liam stood in the empty parking lot without any idea where to search for Alex. He checked his phone, but there were no calls or messages from his boyfriend. Without success, he tried to call him again.

It was cold, and it started to rain again. Liam went back to the car and closed the door. He blew warm air on his cold hands and rubbed them against each other. Then he started the engine and was about to drive home when he saw a car parking at the gas station, and Coach Hanson stepped out.

The man had been Alex's swimming coach. A small spark of hope awoke in Liam's mind. It was a long shot, probably a far long shot, but Liam had to ask if Coach Hanson had seen Alex. He drove to the gas station and parked.

"Hello, sir," Liam said hesitantly. "You might not remember me, but I'm Liam, and I graduated from Fairmont High School last spring."

"Hi … Liam," Coach Hanson said, unsure why Liam was talking to him.

"Um, I'm looking for Alex Wesley. He's my … roommate at Eastwood University, and we arrived in Fairmont yesterday," Liam said. "He went to see his father last night, and I haven't seen him since, so I was wondering if you might have seen him?"

"I'm sorry, but I haven't seen him lately," Coach Hanson said, and the tone of his voice was a bit annoyed.

"I see. Sorry to bother you," Liam said. "I even visited their house at Woodland Avenue, but couldn't find him there." Liam sighed and started to turn away.

"Paul Wesley doesn't live there anymore."

Liam stopped and looked at the coach in confusion. *Did Alex's father move without telling him?* There was something that Liam couldn't understand. Alex hadn't known that his mother had died or his father moved away. And now Alex had mysteriously disappeared, and Liam could read from Coach Hanson's behavior that the man had something against Alex.

It required a lot of persuasion to get Coach Hanson to give him Mr. Wesley's new address, but finally Liam got it. Luckily, Alex's father seemed to live in Fairmont still, and Liam had a rough idea where his new home was. Liam thanked the coach and began to walk toward his car.

"If you find Alex, tell him he should be ashamed that he didn't take part in his mother's funeral," Coach Hanson shouted when Liam was opening the door of his father's car.

"He didn't know she had died," Liam replied, stepped into the car and closed the door.

Liam drove to the suburb where he assumed that the address was. It took him less than ten minutes to locate the apartment building. Many of the houses in the neighborhood hadn't been painted for decades, and the cars that were parked here and there were timeworn.

After parking the car, Liam approached the apartment where Mr. Wesley was supposed to live. Compared to the Wesleys' luxury house on the other side of the city, it felt weird that Alex's father had decided to move here. There were a couple of suspicious men approaching from the opposite direction, and Liam decided to speed up so that he reached Mr. Wesley's door before the men were too close.

Liam knocked on the door and looked to the left. Luckily, the two men hadn't paid him any attention. Then the door was yanked open, and Paul Wesley was standing in front of him. He was dressed in a white t-shirt and boxers. He was drunk, but Liam didn't notice that in his surprise.

"Um, good morning, sir," Liam said. "I'm looking for Alex."

Mr. Wesley looked at Liam and recognized who was standing on his porch. He gave Liam a vague smile and gestured for him to step in.

Chapter 11

Paul Wesley stared at the young man who was standing in the middle of his living room and looking around. The room was full of his dirty clothes and beer bottles, but Paul didn't feel the slightest hint of embarrassment that he hadn't cleaned for Liam's visit.

God had taken his wife away from him in revenge for Paul letting his son become a homo. That was the best explanation Paul had been able to come up with while celebrating Blackout Wednesday with his new best friend: cheap whiskey. And if what he had come to realize was true, the devil himself had just entered his apartment.

"Is Alex here?" Liam asked.

Paul looked at Liam's thin body and boyish face. His voice was soft, and it irritated Paul. Where Alex came across as a real man, the creep in his living room was so evidently a queer.

"Have you fucked my son?" Paul asked, staring hard at Liam.

The boy looked scared and blushed. It was enough of an answer for Paul. That son-of-a-bitch had lured Alex. *My son was straight. He had to be. He was my son. And now I don't have a son anymore*, Paul thought, and the anger inside him kept growing.

"Sir, I believe it's better that I leave," Liam said but didn't move.

Paul was blocking the front door, which was the only exit from the apartment. He had no intention of letting Liam go. He had trapped the devil, and God was finally on his side. It was Thanksgiving Day after all.

"Please, can I go?" Liam asked when Paul didn't budge from the door.

"Aren't you enjoying my company?" Paul said.

He saw Liam looking around the room like he was searching for an escape route. The devil in his apartment was frightened, and it amused Paul. The alcohol he had consumed the whole morning made it hard to think straight, but Paul did his best to stay focused. He might not get another chance.

"I asked you a question, boy," Paul said and took a knife from the dining table.

Liam's face went pale, and he took a couple of steps back until he was in the corner of the room. Paul held the knife in his hand and waited for an answer, which never came.

"Fucking answer me. Have you fucked my son?" Paul yelled.

"Alex and I are dating. We are boyfriends," Liam said. His voice was quiet and scared.

"How the fuck can two boys date each other?" Paul laughed. The whole idea sounded ridiculous to him. "You're nothing but a couple of fags."

"I love Alex," Liam said, and his voice was barely louder than a whisper.

Paul took a step closer to Liam, who was standing with his back against the wall. *The devil has nowhere to escape*, Paul thought and took another step. Having been drinking the whole morning, he felt some urgency to pee, but even his drunken mind told him that the devil would cut and run if he visited the bathroom.

"Please, Mr. Wesley. Let me go," Liam whined.

"You ruined my life!" Paul roared.

The two of them were staring at each other in the small room, and there were less than ten feet between them. Paul had the knife in his right hand, and he was preparing to beat the devil. Liam breathed rapidly and pondered his options for making a break for the door.

Paul attacked, swiping with the knife. It hit Liam on his left arm, not deep but enough to scratch the skin. *I have the devil's blood on my knife*, Paul thought with a wicked smile.

"Please, can we talk?" Liam pleaded.

"Time for talking is over," Paul said, stepping closer.

Liam raised his hands to protect his face and did his best to dodge the drunken man and his knife. He tried to escape, but then Paul shoved him to the floor. The battle was over, and Paul would get his devil. He raised the knife to stab Liam in the back.

"Paul, what the fuck are you doing? Put the knife away!" Thomas Hanson yelled from the door.

"This faggot turned my son a homo," Paul said.

Thomas didn't hesitate. He marched through the room and took the knife from Paul's hand. Then Thomas lifted his friend and put him on the sofa. He gave Paul a look that made it clear that Paul was expected to stay still.

"Are you okay?" Thomas asked Liam, who was shaking on the floor.

"I … I think so," Liam said. Both his arms were bleeding, but the wounds didn't look severe.

Liam thanked Thomas for saving him and left the apartment without looking back. Once Liam had closed the door, Thomas turned toward Paul, who was still sitting on the sofa.

"What on earth is going on in here? And why didn't you tell your son that his mother had died?" Thomas asked.

"I don't have a son," Paul answered bitterly. Then he walked to the bathroom.

It was late afternoon when Paul woke up. It took a while for him to realize where he was, but then he recognized the material of the sofa in his new apartment. Next, he could smell the aroma of fresh coffee, and he noticed Thomas standing by the dining table.

"Feeling better?" Thomas asked. His voice was authoritative.

"A bit," Paul said and rose to sit.

"Then explain why you tried to kill that boy," Thomas ordered.

Paul looked around the room and discovered that it was clean. Thomas must have cleaned it while he was sleeping. *Did I really try to kill him?* Paul asked himself and was shocked by the answer.

"I was drunk," he said and looked at his friend, embarrassed.

"Really? You drink some booze, and then you start killing people," Thomas said. His voice was angry.

The events of the morning were getting clearer and clearer in his head, and Paul had to admit that Thomas had a point. On the other hand, Alex had humiliated him in the worst possible way. Paul felt ashamed to talk about it with Thomas, but he felt that he had to give some explanation for his actions.

"Alex is … gay," he said and looked at Thomas like he was afraid of losing his friend.

"Oh … I didn't expect that," Thomas said. "But why did you try to stab that boy here earlier?

"He's the one who made my son a cocksucker," Paul said and felt his anger growing again. "Do you get it now?"

"No. I don't understand you, Paul," Thomas said.

They were silent for a while. Then Thomas took a mug from the cupboard, filled it with coffee, and gave it to Paul. Without saying a word, he took the cup.

Usually, coffee helped, but this time, he wasn't sure whether he felt any better when the mug was empty.

"So, your son is gay, and that's why you didn't invite him to his mother's funeral," Thomas said.

Paul nodded, hoping that Thomas would finally understand why he was so mad.

"And the boy who visited here this morning is Alex's boyfriend, and you tried to kill him," Thomas continued.

"Um, maybe I was overreacting, but you should see my point now," Paul said.

Thomas stood up. He took a couple of steps around the small room, rubbing his face with his hands. Then he turned to look at Paul.

"You're a monster," Thomas said and walked out of the door.

Chapter 12

It was an ordinary office, very different than Alex had seen in movies and TV series. The police had arrested him, and he had spent the night at the station trying to get some sleep in jail. Now, the female officer had taken him to this room and offered him a cup of coffee.

"Mr. Wesley, can you tell me what happened last night?" the officer said.

"My mom had died, and I was looking for my father," Alex said, "and then I met Rick Donovan at the park."

"Mr. Donovan said that he had been walking in the park when you suddenly, and without any reason, attacked him," the officer read from her notes.

"That's a lie."

"Of course."

Alex had a feeling that the officer didn't believe him. Rick had been nagging until he had lost his temper, and they had started to fight. Alex's hands were covered in bruises, and his stomach hurt. Most likely, Rick wasn't any better.

"He saw me in the park and approached me, calling me … names," Alex said and tried to look as innocent as possible.

"Mr. Donovan used offensive language," the officer said to herself, making notes at the same time. "Which one of you started the fight?"

"He kept harassing me, and then we were on the ground hitting each other," Alex said and looked down. "I might have hit first."

The officer thanked Alex for his honesty and kept writing notes. It had all happened so fast that Alex wasn't sure if she had been there the previous night when he had been arrested. What he could remember was that it had been a young black male officer who had cuffed him and walked him to the police car.

"Mr. Donovan's face looked quite bad, and he's in the hospital right now," the female office on the other side of the table said.

The comment scared Alex, and he could already see himself in an orange jumpsuit. *I need to tell her*, he thought and considered saying something that he had seldom shared with anyone in Fairmont. Actually, those words had come out of his mouth only once, to his mother—and, apparently, that had been a mistake.

"Ma'am, there's something you need to know," Alex said and felt uncomfortable.

The officer looked at him with raised eyebrows.

"Um, I am…. Rick called me…," Alex said, frustrated with how hard it was to get those words out of his mouth.

"I'm gay, and Rick called me a faggot, and half a year ago, he tried to attack my boyfriend with a baseball bat," Alex blurted out.

The police officer looked at him, and Alex was sure that coming out to her made his position only worse. They were in Fairmont, after all. Alex wished he could take his words back. Maybe it was better if it had been just a regular fight between two former high school buddies.

"Is Liam Green your boyfriend?" the officer asked as she checked her papers.

"Yes," Alex said in a shy voice, and his face turned red out of embarrassment.

"I see…. Let me check one thing," the officer said and left the room.

Alex was sure that the officer had left to tell her colleagues that they had arrested a homosexual, and now they were putting their heads together to determine how to maximize his suffering. He had lived most of his life in Fairmont, and he knew how close-minded the people were.

Ten minutes later, the officer returned. She had left all her papers and notes somewhere. Alex wasn't sure whether that was a bad or good sign.

"Mr. Wesley, I hope you understand that an assault is a serious crime," she said and looked Alex in the eyes.

Alex nodded.

"I checked with the hospital, and they said that Mr. Donovan didn't have any permanent injuries," the officer said.

It sounded like good news, but Alex was still holding his breath.

"So, we will let you go, Mr. Wesley, and I hope we don't meet again," she said, "at least under these circumstances."

"You won't press charges?" Alex said, both relieved and surprised.

"Well, that's Mr. Donovan's decision, but I'll talk to him. You shouldn't be worried. I'm sure he doesn't want us to investigate this as a hate crime," she said and smiled at Alex.

She's on my side, Alex realized and felt the urge to hug the officer. He didn't, however. They shook hands, and Alex left the police station, worried that if he stayed there any longer, she would change her mind.

Maybe Liam's right, and most people don't care that I'm gay, Alex thought while walking on the sidewalk toward the park where his car was. Then he realized that Liam must be worried about where he had been. Alex began to jog; he wanted to see his boyfriend as quickly as possible.

Liam's mother put the turkey in the middle of the table and sat down. Alex and Liam had gathered together with Liam's parents in the dining room to celebrate Thanksgiving Day. The fact that Alex had lost his parents was present, and only a few words were said during the meal.

Alex looked at the bandages on Liam's arms and felt guilty. His father had tried to kill his boyfriend. No matter how hard Mr. and Mrs. Green made an effort to convince him that it wasn't his fault, Alex still felt that he was not fully welcome at the table.

Liam had hugged him as soon as he had come from the police station, and Liam's parents had said all those supportive words. Alex could still remember the look on Mrs. Green's face when he had told them that he had spent the night in jail, and he couldn't blame her.

After they had finished dinner, Alex offered to help clear the table and wash the dishes, but Mrs. Green politely declined. He wasn't sure if Mrs. Green just wanted to treat him as a guest or whether she felt uncomfortable being with him in the kitchen. In any case, Alex followed Liam and his father to the living room.

Soon, Liam went to the bathroom, and Alex was alone with Mr. Green. The TV was on, but neither of them was watching it.

"Alex, can I ask you one thing?" Mr. Green began carefully. "Does your father know that you're gay?"

"Um, I think so," Alex said and showed him the text message that he had gotten from his father.

"Oh my God," Mr. Green said as soon as he read it. "I'm so sorry."

"Me, too."

Alex sat on the sofa and did his best to swallow the sadness that was raising in his throat. A tear rolled down his cheek, but he swiped it away before Liam's father could see it. Or maybe he saw it.

"What kind of a father would try to kill…?" Alex began to say, but the words faded away.

He couldn't think of what he would have done if Liam had died. His eyes filled with tears again, and then Alex wasn't able to hold it in anymore. He began to cry, and this time, there was no way Mr. Green couldn't have noticed it. Also, Liam saw it when he came from the bathroom.

"Has something happened?" Liam asked, worried.

"Alex has had terrible two days," his father said and gestured for Liam to comfort Alex.

Liam sat next to Alex, and they hugged for a long time. Alex couldn't speak, but he felt that half of his pain and sorrow disappeared when Liam held him and petted his hair. They kissed briefly, which brought a small smile to Alex's face.

"Alex, just remember that Jenny and I will do anything to support you," Mr. Green said. "You're like our son. We would even adopt you."

"Yuck, please don't. Dating my brother would be too weird," Liam said.

They all laughed.

Mrs. Green came from the kitchen carrying a tray with four ice cream bowls. As soon as they had their desserts, Liam leaned against Alex on the sofa and Alex put his arm around Liam's shoulders. He noticed that Liam's parents had taken the same position on the other sofa.

While it felt cozy, Alex was painfully aware that they could have never sat like this around his parents. And now it was too late anyway.

Alex and Liam packed the car on the Sunday after Thanksgiving. Classes at Eastwood University would continue on Monday for another two weeks before the exam period, which was followed by Christmas break. After saying goodbye to Liam's parents, they hit the road.

They had driven hardly half a mile when Alex slowed down and looked at his boyfriend. "Tell me how to get to my father's house," he said.

"No. You can't mean—"

"Please. I need to see my father."

Ten minutes later, Alex parked the car near the red brick building behind which his father's apartment was. He asked Liam to lock the door and wait in the car. Liam happily agreed, as he had no intention of seeing that evil man anytime soon. It was bad enough that Alex was going there.

Alex walked behind the corner and approached his father's apartment slowly. All his muscles were tense, and his heart began to beat faster. Somebody was sitting on the porch, and since Alex could see only his back, he wasn't sure who he was but assumed it had to be his father.

Just when Alex was about to enter the small yard in front of the apartment, he saw his father coming from the door, carrying two bottles of beer. Quickly, Alex crouched behind the low fence. His father was too focused on the drinks to notice him.

Those few seconds when Alex had been looking at his father had created an image that would stay in his mind forever. The man hadn't washed his hair or clothes for weeks. His greasy hair was accompanied by a puffy face and grayish stubble.

Is that bum my father? Alex asked himself, shocked, and saw how the men opened the beer bottles.

"Down the hatch," Alex heard the other man saying.

"To the lonely men," his father added.

From his hiding place, Alex saw how his father tried to sit on the cheap plastic seat on the porch. He took hold of the wall and spilled half of the beer on his lap. The old man cursed, and even though his choice of words wasn't the most innovative, his drinking buddy laughed loudly.

"You look like you pissed your pants," the other man blurted.

"Like anybody would care," Alex's father said bitterly. "My wife's in Heaven and that cocksucker son of hers will rot in Hell."

"Lord gives, and Lord takes," the other man said, and they both laughed.

Alex couldn't listen anymore. He knew that the alcohol was talking, but it was also a man he had considered his father for eighteen years. Alex stood up and looked at the two men who were bumbling around on the porch on a Sunday morning. He entered the yard, and the men saw him.

"Dad," Alex said and looked his father in the eyes. His mother had promised to pay his tuition at Eastwood, and Alex had hoped he could persuade his father to respect her promise. Now his optimism was rapidly fading away, but he had to try.

"Get the fuck out of here! You're not my son," his father said and tried to stand up but fell on the ground.

Pissed off, Alex turned around and rushed toward his Mustang. He was crossing the road to get to the sidewalk on the other side when he heard a car braking to his left. He just caught sight of the black SUV approaching him and the scared woman behind the wheel. Then the car hit him.

Chapter 13

Everything was white, and the smell of disinfectant filled the room. Doctor Mark Goodfellow took the medical report and checked what the night nurse had written. Then he approached the patient and checked his eyes with a small flashlight. With a concerned look on his face, he left the room.

If you've seen one brain injury, you've seen one brain injury, Dr. Goodfellow thought, knowing that every case was unique. Some signs or symptoms were evident soon after the traumatic event, while one might become aware of the others weeks later. Still, it worried him that the patient had been in a coma almost a week.

He passed the coffee room and saw the medical superintendent coming from the elevators. The old lady was a recognized professional, and over the years, Dr.

Goodfellow had learned from her a lot more than they taught about neurosurgery at medical school.

"How's the young man in room seventeen?" she asked.

"I just checked him. Unfortunately, still in the coma," Dr. Goodfellow said.

"You want me to talk to the family?" she asked.

"Thanks, but I can do that," he said.

Dr. Goodfellow pressed the button and took the elevator to the first floor. The family in the lobby recognized him immediately and stood up. He could see from their faces that they were prepared for the bad news.

"He's still in the coma," Dr. Goodfellow said. "We've given him different medicines, but so far he's not reacting to any of them."

"But Shawn will wake up, right?" Scott said.

"Unfortunately, we can only wait and see," Dr. Goodfellow said as empathically as he could.

"If he wakes up, how likely is it that he'll be okay?" Scott's father asked.

"Mr. Abrahamson, your son's skull was fractured, and there was a hematoma between his brain and dura mater, which is the meninx closest to the skull," Dr. Goodfellow explained.

"But you said you operated on it, and everything should be fine," Mr. Abrahamson said.

"The operation was successful," Dr. Goodfellow said with some pride in his voice. "However, the hematoma was quite large, and it might have damaged parts of his brain. I wish I had some answers, but we will know only when he wakes up. If he wakes up."

Scott left the lobby. He had to go for a walk. Mr. and Mrs. Abrahamson sat down, and Dr. Goodfellow explained to them that the hematoma had been in the primary motor cortex that controls muscle movements.

"Is it possible that he's paralyzed?" Mrs. Abrahamson asked, scared.

"Everything is possible, but that is not very likely," Dr. Goodfellow said.

Both of the parents sighed. Under other circumstances, Dr. Goodfellow might have found the simultaneous reaction hilarious.

"Typical symptoms are muscle weakness and involuntary muscle twitches, which can be either temporary or permanent," Dr. Goodfellow said.

"That doesn't sound too bad, does it?" Mrs. Abrahamson said.

"In the best case, Shawn should be able to live a normal life," Dr. Goodfellow said, "but I don't want to give you any promises before he's awake."

Scott returned to the lobby and found his parents sitting there. As none of them had eaten for hours, they walked to the cafeteria. Mrs. Abrahamson bought them coffee and sandwiches, and they sat down at a table near a group of houseplants.

"Have you heard anything from the cops?" Scott asked.

"They have talked with the boys who pushed Shawn down the stairs," Scott's father said. "Luckily, there are plenty of people who saw it."

"I've been thinking about it a lot, and I still can't understand why this happened to my son," Mrs. Abrahamson said, and a single tear ran down her left cheek.

Her husband took hold of her hand and tried to reassure her that it hadn't been Shawn's fault and that the boy would soon be okay. Scott looked at his parents and thought about whether he should tell them that Shawn had been bullied for years, and he believed he knew the reason.

"I think I know why they keep harassing Shawn," Scott said finally.

"You do?" his mother said and looked at Mr. Abrahamson.

Scott nodded. Suddenly, he felt that it was not his place to out his brother. Besides, he wasn't even sure if Shawn was gay. His brother had been avoiding the topic even though Scott had tried to lead the discussion in that direction a couple of times.

"Um, I think...," Scott began, thinking of a way to take back what he had just said, "Shawn might be ... gay." As soon as the words left his mouth, he felt guilty.

"If he was, what would you think about it?" his mother asked.

Surprised by the question, Scott was quiet for a moment. He looked at his parents, who were both waiting for his answer. *Is this some kind of test?* Scott thought. Would his parents be disappointed if Scott didn't mind that his brother might be gay?

"Um, to be honest, it wouldn't matter to me," Scott said, prepared to defend his opinion. "Actually, two of my best friends at college are a gay couple," he added.

Scott was nervous as he waited for his parents' reaction. His brother was fighting for his life, and he had just revealed that he was hanging around with two gay guys, and his brother might be one, too. He regretted that he had opened his mouth.

"You're right," Mrs. Abrahamson said finally. "Shawn came out to us after you left for college."

"He did?" Scott said.

"Well, I'm his mother. I had known it for a long time," she said with a small smile.

"Why didn't you tell me?" Scott asked.

"It wasn't our place to tell you," his father said. "If you haven't noticed, Shawn idolizes you. He was so scared that you wouldn't approve."

Even though he could understand his little brother's apprehension, Scott couldn't help feeling a bit hurt that Shawn had told their parents but not to him. Was it his being a jock that made people assume that he had problems with gays?

"I guess you are okay with it?" Scott asked.

"You thought that we wouldn't be?" his mother said.

Scott blushed. Indeed, he had assumed his parents were a bit more conservative, and it still surprised him that Shawn had told them. Scott would have wanted to know more, but he thought that it was best to discuss the matter with his brother as soon as he woke from the coma. If he ever did.

"One more thing," Scott's father said. "It would be good if you didn't mention to Shawn that you know about him. You should let him tell you when he's ready."

Scott nodded and hoped he would get a chance to talk with Shawn soon.

Tyler hugged him as soon as Scott entered their dorm room. It was Monday evening, and their lectures would continue the following morning, which meant that Scott had had to leave Austin and return to Eddington even though his brother hadn't awakened yet. Luckily, his parents would be there with him as soon as he opened his eyes.

"I'm so sorry about your brother," Tyler said and kept his arms wrapped around his roommate.

Scott hugged him back, and they stood there, maybe far too long for two jocks, but Scott didn't mind. He just hoped that Shawn would soon be okay, and the comfort that he got from Tyler felt good. He couldn't have wished for a better roommate.

"Thanks, man," Scott said. "Good to see you."

"If there's anything I can do, just let me know," Tyler said and finally let go of his friend.

"Thanks," Scott said, and his eyes filled with tears as he thought of his brother.

"Here," Tyler said, passing Scott a box of tissues. "Those are clean. I tossed the ones I used for wanking."

Scott laughed. Certainly, he was lucky to have Tyler as his roommate. No matter where their path would go after college, they would be life-long friends, which was yet another benefit of college.

"I was right about Shawn. He's gay," Scott said.

"How do you know? Isn't he still in a… coma?" Tyler asked, surprised.

"My parents kind of told me," Scott said and repeated their discussion to Tyler.

"Breaking news: a white Christian couple from Austin, Texas, came out as supporters of the gay community," Tyler mimicked a CNN news anchor.

Scott laughed even though he had to admit that he hadn't expected his parents' positive reaction. On the other hand, his brother had assumed that he wouldn't be cool about it, either. *What does that say about our family?* Scott thought.

"They know who did it?" Tyler asked.

"Yeah. It was a group of high school seniors," Scott said.

"What's going to happen to them?"

"Depends on whether they investigate it as an assault or homicide."

Tyler was silent for a moment. Then the message sank in, and he realized that Scott's brother might not survive the attack. He didn't know Shawn and had never met him, but he still felt anger for those guys who had done it

Scott's phone began ringing. He didn't recognize the number but answered anyways. The caller was a freelance reporter preparing an article for the *Austin American-Statesman* newspaper, and after confirming that

Scott was Shawn's brother, she went directly to business.

"Your brother is a victim of a horrible hate crime. How does it feel?" she asked.

"Um, horrible, I guess," Scott said, confused.

"You must have visited your brother at the hospital, right? Can you describe his injuries?" she continued with the same enthusiasm.

"Look, I really don't want to talk about this," Scott said.

"I understand that you are shocked by these horrible events, but don't you think your brother deserves for everyone to know what he's going through?" she said. "So, is he severely injured?"

Scott hung up the call, feeling annoyed. Soon, the phone started to ring again, but he declined the call and switched off the phone. He looked at Tyler and told him that it had been a reporter who was trying to profit from his family's situation.

"Fucking vulture," Tyler muttered.

"Have you heard from Alex and Liam?" Scott asked to change the subject.

"No, nothing," Tyler said. "I got here around noon and didn't see Alex's car in the parking lot."

"Let's go and check. I'm starving. Maybe they'll join us for dinner somewhere," Scott said.

Tyler changed into jeans, and they walked the short distance to the dorm where Alex's and Liam's room was. Some students had gathered to watch TV in the second floor hall, and there was another group playing some board game.

Scott knocked on the door, and soon he heard some movement inside. Liam came to open the door and let Scott and Tyler into the small room. Tyler looked around, but couldn't see their other friend anywhere.

"Where's Alex?" he asked.

Chapter 14

Alex flushed the toilet and walked to the sink to wash his hands. His left hip was still a bit sore where the car had hit him, and his hands and arms had small bruises. Luckily, the woman had not been driving fast.

What hurt most was that his father had not called an ambulance or even come to see what had happened. Alex could remember the two men laughing on the porch when he had been lying in the street. The scared woman had driven him to the health clinic where they had checked him and let him go soon after.

When Alex returned to his room, he saw Scott and Tyler there. As soon as Alex had closed the door, Tyler stood up and approached him, opening his arms.

"I heard about your mother. I'm so sorry," Tyler said and hugged Alex.

Alex felt Tyler patting his back, and it felt comforting. Tyler was a bit taller than Alex, and his strong arms kept Alex in a tight grip. Alex was happy that the jock felt comfortable enough to be around him, even hug him, although he knew that Alex was gay.

Don't always put yourself down. People don't automatically hate you, Alex heard Liam's words in his mind and took a stronger hold of Tyler.

"I'm sorry for your loss," Scott said as he hugged Alex briefly.

"Thanks, man," Alex said. "Um, how is your brother?" he added tentatively.

Alex had heard about Shawn from Scott just before the holidays when Scott was leaving for Austin. Alex had planned to call Scott after Thanksgiving, but then the events in Fairmont had given him other things to worry about, and he had never made the call.

"Long story short, in a coma in the hospital," Scott said sadly.

"Oh, I didn't realize it was that bad," Alex said.

"Don't worry. You've had enough troubles anyway," Scott said. "So, why don't you join us for some supper, and I'll tell you the rest of the story?"

"Sure, I'm starving," Liam said and pulled his jacket from the rack.

"Um, I think I'll pass. I'm too tired," Alex said, looking uncomfortable, "but you should go."

The expression on Liam's face was a bit puzzled, but he assumed that Alex wanted to be alone after losing his parents. After making sure that Alex was okay, he left the room with Scott and Tyler.

Can't he understand that I don't have money to eat supper in some restaurant? Alex thought bitterly as soon as Liam had closed the door. He hadn't received any money from his parents after his mother had died, and after meeting his father, Alex's hopes of him paying his tuition and other fees were not high.

Feeling hungry, he opened the fridge, only to realize that it was pretty much empty. They didn't have any bread, but Alex ate peanut butter straight from the jar. It was sweet, but after the fifth spoonful, it began to taste disgusting. Unfortunately, the only alternative would have been the orange marmalade, so he closed the fridge and took water from the tap. At least that was free.

The tuition for undergraduates at Eddington University was twenty-seven-thousand dollars a year. As it was split into nine portions, Alex was expected to pay three-thousand dollars every month from September to May. In addition, he had to pay five-hundred dollars for the room every month.

There's no fucking way I can find a job that would pay me that much money, Alex wallowed in agony.

Even without the financial troubles, Alex's studies had not proceeded as well as he had wished. In addition to the failed chemistry course, the content of the signal processing introduction course sounded like Hebrew to him. Alex picked up his textbook and tried to understand the Fourier transformation that the professor had explained before the holiday break.

After a couple of attempts to understand the theory of periodic functions and their integration domains,

Alex threw the book on the floor. *What's the point? My studies are over anyway*, he thought. He lay on the bed, his stomach growling so badly that he could have eaten a horse.

"Here you are," the waitress said as she set the bacon and double cheese hamburger in front of Liam.

"Thanks. Looks delicious," Liam said and added ketchup on his French fries.

Scott and Tyler got their burgers, too, and the three of them began to eat with good appetites. Alex and Liam had spent most of the day driving from Fairmont, and Liam couldn't understand why Alex hadn't joined them in the restaurant. On the other hand, Liam could understand that his mother having died and losing his father must have upset Alex. Maybe it was good to give Alex some space.

Liam was worried, though. Alex had been silent, even absent-minded, during their visit in Fairmont, which was understandable, but every time Liam tried to talk about Alex's parents, he had avoided the discussion and turned the topic elsewhere.

Maybe he needs time to process things, Liam thought, knowing that his boyfriend was magnificent at keeping things inside him.

"So, you said that your brother is in a coma," Liam said, shifting his focus to his friends.

"Some guys from his class attacked him after school," Scott said. "It was a week ago on Tuesday."

"He's been unconscious almost a week?" Liam asked, shocked.

Scott nodded. He told Liam and Tyler how the family had visited the hospital daily, and every day the hope of Shawn's full recovery was getting thinner and thinner. Liam could see that Scott was grieved, which didn't surprise him.

"Was it because he might be…?" Liam began to ask.

"Gay," Scott said. "The kids who saw what happened heard them calling him a faggot before they pushed him down the stairs."

Liam felt sick. He could remember far too well how the other boys in high school had given him similar treatment. The worst of his enemies had been Rick, Alex's former best friend, who had tried to hit him with a baseball bat. Liam didn't want to think about what might have happened if his friend, Tristan, hadn't come to rescue him.

"Are you offended that I said the word … faggot?" Scott said, and looked apologetic. "I didn't mean it like that. I was just repeating what they said."

"No. Don't worry about it," Liam said. "I was just thinking about my time in high school."

"Some people are idiots," Tyler said.

They finished their burgers, and Scott told his friends that Shawn had come out to their parents. He also mentioned that he wasn't supposed to know it. Liam wished that Scott and Shawn would get a chance to talk about it as he knew how painful it was to keep something so fundamental a secret.

"When you started dating, how did you know that Alex was gay?" Tyler asked.

"Um, we were just friends at first," Liam said. "Then Alex found gay porn on my laptop," he added and blushed.

Tyler laughed. "Quite an obvious clue."

Liam could remember the events in Alex's room clearly. They had been studying on Alex's bed, and suddenly the jock had jumped to the other side of the room like he had been bitten by a snake. Now, he could laugh at it, but at that time, it had been one of the most embarrassing moments in his life.

"I hope your brother will be okay," Liam said to Scott, "and just let me know if there's anything I can do."

"Thanks, man," Scott said and smiled at Liam.

When Liam returned to their dorm room an hour later, Alex was distant and silent. Liam hugged his boyfriend but felt that the response wasn't very enthusiastic. Alex wrapped his arms around him but didn't even kiss him. As both of them were tired from traveling, they went to bed. This time, there was no cuddling as Alex turned his back to Liam and closed his eyes.

"Good night, honey," Liam said, unsure if he should do something to make his boyfriend feel better.

Alex muttered something and switched off the lamp.

After a night of poor sleep, the alarm clock went off far too early. Lying on the bed next to him, Alex saw Liam smiling and waiting for a hug. Alex turned his head in the other direction and stood up. Taking his towel from the chair back, he left for the shower without saying a word.

Alex was still angry at Liam for going to the restaurant with his friends the previous night. *Scott barely had to ask, and he was already going out with them. He should've understood I don't have much money*, Alex thought while walking to the shower room.

All of the eight showers were taken, and Alex had to wait his turn a while. He looked at the students who were washing and chatting happily with each other and realized that soon he would not be here. Alex didn't have money for the December tuition fee or his rent, and he couldn't even pay back the money that Liam had loaned him.

Where the fuck am I going to live? Alex asked himself after realizing that his father would not welcome him to his new apartment.

"Alex, the shower is free," someone shouted.

Awakening from his thoughts, Alex looked in the direction of the voice and saw the guy living in the adjacent room walking toward him. Forcing a smile on his face, Alex walked to the shower and began washing his body and hair.

After both of them had dressed, Alex and Liam walked to the nearby student canteen for breakfast. Liam's jaw dropped in amazement when he saw the enormous pile of food that Alex carried from the buffet table.

"You must be hungry," Liam said.

"Um, yeah," Alex said.

Those were the only words they said to each other during breakfast. When they walked back to their room, Alex felt uneasiness in his stomach. He had intended to eat enough so that he could skip lunch and save some money, but too much was simply too much.

"I need to see the Dean," Alex said and turned left when they approached the front door of the dorm.

"Okay. Why?" Liam said.

Alex didn't answer. He just shrugged and walked away. It wasn't fair to Liam, and Alex should have realized that, but right now, he couldn't think straight.

Dean Curtis was busy, and her secretary proposed to schedule a meeting for the next week. Alex explained his issue, and the secretary called the Director of Admission and Financial Aid.

"Mrs. Mason is available in fifteen minutes," the secretary said after she had finished the short call. "Turn right, and you'll find her office at the end of the corridor."

Half an hour later, a fat woman opened the door and asked Alex to come into her office. They shook hands, and Mrs. Mason waddled back to her chair and sat down.

"How can I help you?" she asked, typing on her computer at the same time.

"I have some financial problems," Alex said.

"Don't we all?" Mrs. Mason said before looking up at Alex.

The discussion hadn't started as well as Alex would have wanted. He took a better position in his seat and told the director how his mother had died, and his father didn't have money to pay for his studies. It was only partially true, but Alex hoped it was good enough.

"I'm sorry to hear that, Mr. Wesley," Mrs. Mason said, and for a short moment, she looked sincere.

"What options do I have?" Alex asked.

Mrs. Mason looked at Alex like she was shopping for an evening dress and had found the worst costume in the world. She went through the alternatives from finding a rich relative to taking a student loan, but Alex didn't find any of them suitable for his situation.

"How about a scholarship?" Alex asked. "I'm a swimmer."

"Humph, I can see that you have failed one of the mandatory courses so the academic scholarship is out of the question anyways," Mrs. Mason said and read something from the screen of his computer. "So, you're in the swim club?"

Alex nodded and held his breath.

"I'm sorry, Mr. Wesley. We have a scholarship program for varsity team members only," she said and looked Alex in the eyes.

Alex sighed. Apparently, his college career had come to an end, and he didn't have any idea what he would do next. Eastwood University was a private school, which didn't have a place for a poor, mediocre student like him.

"So, what are the next steps?" Alex asked, admitting his defeat.

"If I understood correctly, you don't have money to pay your tuition and room cost for December," Mrs. Mason said.

"That's correct, ma'am," Alex said.

"Well, you can finish your courses and take the exams. If you decide to apply to another college, we can transfer your credits there," she said.

"How long can I stay in the room?"

"Until Christmas break. There are students waiting for a dorm room, and I want to give your room to the first on the waiting list as soon as possible."

Hearing her words felt bad, but considering that Alex didn't have money, the arrangement was actually rather fair. He could take part in learning and live in the small room for free one more month. In that same amount of time, he would have to find a new apartment, and the only thing that was sure was that he would not become his father's roommate.

Alex thanked Mrs. Mason for her time and left the office. He walked out of the building and felt the cold wind against his face. Dozens of students were coming from the dorms and were now on their way to the buildings all over campus. The professors would soon start their lectures, and everything would continue as it was supposed to, except for Alex.

I need to talk to Liam, Alex thought and regretted that he hadn't told his boyfriend any of his problems. Liam didn't know that he had failed the chemistry course, not to mention his lack of money to continue his studies. Liam was a straight-A student, and Alex was worried that he wouldn't want to date a loser like him.

He deserves better, Alex thought and opened the front door of the dorm.

The hall was empty as all the students had already left for their classes. On the corner, there were two sofas where he and Liam had sat together with Tyler and Scott, sharing their experiences after the first two weeks at college.

Suddenly, Alex remembered the childish argument about supper and felt embarrassed. *Like Liam eating with our friends was my biggest problem*, Alex thought as he took the key from his pocket. He opened the door and was surprised to find Liam in their room.

"We need to talk," Liam said, and his face was severe.

"Yes, we do," Alex said.

Chapter 15

Shawn Abrahamson opened his eyes and saw a man and a woman, both wearing funny clothes. He wasn't sure where he was but had a feeling that he had been sleeping, even though he felt extraordinarily tired. The bed wasn't his own, and the people in the room, who were now approaching him, were not his parents.

"Good morning, I'm Dr. Goodfellow, and you are in a hospital," the man said.

"Can you remember your name?" the woman asked.

"Um, Shawn. I'm Shawn Abrahamson," Shawn said.

Why wouldn't I remember my name? Shawn thought and tried to raise his head to see the room and people in there better. Then it hit him, the worst headache ever. Shawn groaned and put his head back on the pillow. Luckily, it helped.

"Careful, don't move your head," Dr. Goodfellow said.

Excellent advice. Like I hadn't realized it.

"Do you remember what happened to you?" the woman asked.

Shawn rolled his eyes. *Why is she asking all these questions?*

An image of the events at school appeared in his mind. His geography class had ended, and he was packing his stuff at his locker when Oliver and Jake had come to mouth off to him. He had made some smartass comment, and the next thing he could remember was when they had pushed him on the stairs.

"I was in a fight," Shawn said and realized that he couldn't remember what had happened next.

He was about to ask how long he had been in the hospital when his right arm twitched and hit the metal frame of the bed. First, it scared Shawn, and then he wanted to swear from the pain. Soon, his arm made another movement, which he didn't seem to be able to control. Confused, he looked at the doctor.

"What's wrong with my arm?" Shawn asked.

"Your skull was wounded rather severely," Dr. Goodfellow said. "We had to operate on your brain in the area that controls your muscle movements."

Shawn took hold of his right hand's wrist to stop the arm from moving. Apparently, his left hand seemed to be in better control. The headache was coming back; fortunately, it wasn't as bad as a moment ago when he had tried to raise his head.

"Will this stop?" Shawn asked, holding his arm, afraid that it would jerk again.

"I can't make you any promises. There are some medicines that might help," Dr. Goodfellow said.

The woman, whom Shawn assumed to be a nurse, fastened the arm to a holder, which she connected to the bed. It allowed him to move the arm but prevented vigorous movements.

"I'll let your parents know that you have awakened. Unfortunately, the police want to talk to you before you can see your parents," Dr. Goodfellow said and left the room.

It took almost an hour for the police officers to arrive, but Shawn was happy as soon as he saw them entering the room. The nurse who had visited the room every five minutes had started to annoy him already. The older police officer offered his hand for shaking before he noticed that Shawn's hand was hanging in the air. He pulled his hand back quickly and cleared his throat.

"Mr. Abrahamson, we would like to ask some questions if that's okay with you," the officer said.

"Sure," Shawn said and stared at the younger officer who had a muscular body and a super cute face. *My pleasure.*

"Could you please describe what happened after you left…," the older officer said and checked his papers, "after you left geography?"

Shawn explained the events to the officers, looking now and then at the younger officer's face and chest. Every time their eyes met, he smiled at the officer in a way that made the man blush slightly. The older police officer, entirely oblivious of the flirting, wrote notes and asked more questions about a couple of details.

"Thanks a lot, Mr. Abrahamson," the older officer said. "I have one more question: why do you think those boys attacked you?"

Before Shawn could answer, his right arm twitched a couple of times. He was embarrassed that he couldn't control it. The officers didn't seem to mind but waited for his answer patiently.

"Well, they think I'm gay, and you know … they had problems with that," Shawn said and looked one more time at the sexy man sitting on the other side of his bed.

The officers thanked Shawn and left the room. Shawn couldn't help staring at the younger man, whose tight blue uniform emphasized his muscular chest and perfect butt. Without the problem with his other arm, the visit would have been great.

Shawn's thoughts shifted to Jamal. *I was on my way to meet him when it happened*, he recalled and realized that it was likely nobody had told his boyfriend why he hadn't showed up to their date or where he had been all this time.

I need to call him. Shawn panicked and tried to look for his phone. He couldn't find it anywhere, but his arm began to twitch again, and Shawn had to stop searching and focus on getting his arm back in control.

A couple of hours later, the somewhat awkward meeting with his parents was over. As Shawn had expected, his mother had been nearly hysterical when she had seen her son lying with his eyes open on the bed. Of course, Shawn understood that not every mother had to wait a week for her child to wake from a coma.

Shawn's mother had, however, confirmed that she had told Jamal what had happened to him. That information calmed Shawn significantly, and he was now eagerly waiting to see Jamal.

Shawn was still lying on the bed, and Dr. Goodfellow was running some tests on him. Moving his head didn't cause as much discomfort as earlier in the morning, but Shawn kept his head strictly on the pillow as he didn't want to risk the sharp pain coming back.

"Raise your right leg," Dr. Goodfellow commanded, and Shawn followed the instructions.

"And now your left," the doctor said.

Unfortunately, even Shawn could feel the difference. The muscles in his right leg had worked fine even though Dr. Goodfellow had kept his hand on Shawn's ankle and pushed down when he had raised his leg. The left leg had moved but was significantly weaker.

"Is there something wrong with my muscles? Should I go to the gym?" Shawn tried to joke even though he wasn't sure how severe the situation was.

"The problem is not in your muscles," Dr. Goodfellow said. "It's in your brain."

The smile faded from Shawn's face. The doctor explained how the muscles of his left leg weren't getting proper instructions from his brain through the nervous system.

But I am telling my leg to raise, Shawn rationalized and tried to give more determined orders for his lower limbs.

"Will I be able to walk?" Shawn asked, realizing that his current condition might have severe symptoms.

"We need to wait until the pressure of your brain fluid decreases. I think we can test walking tomorrow," Dr. Goodfellow said.

"Could I still get your medical opinion today?" Shawn said, sounding desperate. He looked at the doctor with his big green eyes. "Please."

"Your legs have a normal sense of touch, and you can move them. Those are good signs," the doctor said. "However, right now, your left leg might not be strong enough for walking, I'm afraid."

Shawn's right arm twitched, and he had to take hold of the arm with his other hand to stop it moving. The dystonia, as the doctor had called his movement disorder, wasn't getting any better despite the drugs that Shawn had got after the police officers had left. Maybe he was just too impatient.

Great. I'll be a crippled, quivering queer, Shawn thought and sucked his lips into his mouth. Dr. Goodfellow saw the expression on Shawn's face and, on his way out of the room, gave Shawn a comforting smile before asking him to rest.

Shawn pulled his right hand through the loop that the nurse had set up on top of his bed. Every now and then, he felt his hand moving when he tried to get some sleep. It was surprising how tired he was, keeping in mind that he had just slept several days.

Later in the afternoon, Shawn woke up when the nurse came to the room with a tray. The smell of the hot chicken soup, which was flavored with curry, reminded him how hungry he was.

"Thanks," Shawn said when the nurse set the tray in front of him on a small table that was connected to his bed.

The nurse smiled when the boy began to eagerly spoon the soup into his mouth. Shawn took the water glass and was about to drink from it when his arm twitched, spilling the water all over his bed and clothes. Embarrassed, Shawn tried to set the glass back on the tray and succeeded only when he helped with his left hand.

"Sorry," Shawn said in a small voice.

"Don't worry. I'll get you a new glass and a dry blanket," the nurse said. "Maybe you should eat with your left hand."

What a brilliant idea. Like I hadn't realized that already, Shawn thought but just gave the nurse a weak smile.

Ten minutes later, the nurse came back with a new water glass and a blanket. By that time, Shawn had finished his soup even though eating with his left hand had been significantly more challenging. As soon as Shawn had drunk the water, the nurse took the tray and walked toward the door.

"Um, I need some help," Shawn said and blushed slightly.

The nurse stopped and turned to look at him.

"I need to use the restroom," Shawn said.

"Number one or two?"

"One."

The nurse put the tray on the table and opened the cabinet near the door. She didn't find what she was looking for, and she had to open a couple of storage closets more before she found it.

"You can use this," she said and gave Shawn a bedpan.

"Um, thanks," Shawn said and looked at the nurse.

"Yes, sure. I'll give you some privacy," she said and left, closing the door behind her.

This is so embarrassing, Shawn thought as he placed himself in a proper position to empty his bladder. Monitoring that nobody was coming in from the door, he completed the task and put the pisspot on the table. Hoping that the nurse would empty it when he was sleeping, Shawn closed his eyes. Ten minutes later, the Sandman came for a visit.

Shawn's parents visited again later in the afternoon, and after they had left, Shawn took the book that his mother had brought with her and began reading it. He had hardly progressed to the second page when he heard a knock on the door.

"Jamal!" Shawn said with a broad smile on his face.

"Hi, how're you?" Jamal said and approached Shawn slowly.

"Better and better," Shawn said.

Something in Jamal's behavior told Shawn that everything wasn't okay. He was used to his boyfriend being silent and calm, but his usual smile was missing. Worse, Jamal was avoiding eye contact with him.

"Is something wrong?" Shawn asked.

Jamal nodded but said nothing.

"Tell me, baby," Shawn said. "What is it?"

"Seeing you in that bed makes me feel like a complete jerk saying this," Jamal said and swallowed, "but I think we should stop seeing each other. At least, for a while," he added.

Shawn's right arm began twitching, and once again, he had to use his other hand to stop it. Jamal's announcement had come out of blue, and it started to gradually sink in. His boyfriend wanted to break up.

"But why?" Shawn asked, not knowing whether he was surprised, disappointed or angry.

"They are writing about you in newspapers almost every day," Jamal said.

"About me? Why?" Shawn asked, confused.

"Those two guys are being charged with a hate crime. You're some sort of Matthew Shepard two-point-zero or something," Jamal said. "Luckily, you didn't die," he added.

Jamal felt more uncomfortable than maybe ever during his life. He felt the urge to touch Shawn, at least hold his hand, but wasn't sure how Shawn would react after what he had just said. Hence, he just looked at his toes and tried to hold back his tears.

"Shit," Shawn said.

It took a while for Shawn to comprehend that his story was big news in Austin and for most Texans. What he couldn't understand was why Jamal was so upset about the attack being reported in the media.

Then he realized that Jamal had been speaking about a hate crime.

"Wait, did they report my name and that I'm gay?" Shawn asked.

Jamal nodded, and suddenly everything was clear for Shawn. Because of his grandmother, Jamal was too afraid to date an out gay guy.

"Can you forgive me?" Jamal said, and his voice was barely louder than a whisper.

Shawn looked at the cute and kind boy, feeling nothing but emptiness. A teardrop rolled out of his left eye when he nodded lightly. Crying and ashamed, Jamal left the room.

It was too good to be true, Shawn thought and looked at the ceiling. His arm twitched once, but he didn't care.

Chapter 16

Alex sat on his bed and tried to calm down. Liam was waiting for an explanation of his recent behavior, and Alex couldn't blame him for that. He knew he owed it to his boyfriend.

"I can see that something is bothering you," Liam said softly and sat next to Alex.

"They kicked me out of school," Alex said, studying his shoes.

"What? Who? Why?"

"I don't have any money."

Feeling embarrassed, Alex explained to Liam how his father had stopped paying his tuition after his mother had died. His revelation was met with stunned silence, especially after he told Liam that he couldn't get a scholarship even though the administrators knew about his mother's death.

"Will you inherit any money from your mother?" Liam asked.

Alex shook his head. "They had a will. Father gets everything," he said.

"Shit. Why didn't I realize this earlier?" Liam said.

"I should have told you," Alex said. "I'm sorry."

They hugged each other, and it felt so good that neither of them wanted to let go. When they finally pulled apart and Liam saw Alex's face, he realized that this discussion was not only whether Alex could take classes. This was much more.

"They won't let you live here?" Liam said, afraid of the answer.

"I can stay until Christmas," Alex said and looked miserable.

"That's only a couple of weeks."

"I know. And after that, I have nowhere to go."

Renting a small apartment near Eastwood University would have been one option, but without a degree from college, Alex wasn't likely to find a well-paid job. Also, Liam didn't like the idea that Alex would have to sacrifice his future because of him.

"You should apply to a community college," Liam said.

"But that means we can't live together," Alex said.

"I know, but you need a degree," Liam said.

Alex sighed. Liam was right, of course, but his best chances to get into a community college were in Fairmont, and returning there wasn't at the top of his wish list. He knew he would bump into his former high school classmates there, and there were plenty of them he never wanted to meet ever again.

"This sucks," Liam said.

"I wish my mother was still alive," Alex said and turned to look at his boyfriend. "I don't wanna lose you," he said, and his eyes were moist.

Liam hugged him. "You're not going to lose me. We will survive this."

It was already late when Liam returned to their dorm room. After his last lecture, he had visited the nearby grocery store to fill the fridge. Liam assumed that Alex had skipped his classes, which worried Liam, but he decided to say nothing.

"I bought us some food," Liam said as he put the shopping bag on the small kitchen table.

"Thanks," Alex said, helping Liam in unpacking.

Alex felt awkward. He knew that Liam had bought much more than usual just because he didn't have any money. He couldn't pay him back, and they both knew it but said nothing. Liam just smiled when Alex put the prepackaged cheeseburger into the microwave.

Liam's phone began to ring just as the microwave dinged to announce that Alex's dinner was ready. Liam sat down on his bed and answered the call.

"Hi, Mom," Liam said cheerfully. "Actually, I was just about to call you," he added and gave Alex a meaningful look.

Alex nodded. He guessed what Liam wanted to discuss with his mother.

"So nice to hear your voice. I just wanted to check when you and Alex are coming to Fairmont for Christmas break," Liam's mother said enthusiastically. Apparently, she was already missing her son and his boyfriend.

"Um, I have some bad news," Liam said.

"Oh, have you and Alex broken up?"

"No, no. Nothing like that."

Liam could hear the relief in his mother's voice, but it didn't last long. He explained Alex's situation to her and listened as she repeated it to his father. For a while, his parents were talking to each other, and then his mother returned on the line.

"Just talked with your dad, and we were wondering if it would be okay with you if Alex moved into your old room?" she said.

"Thanks, Mom," Liam said with a rush of relief. He was happy that his boyfriend would at least have a roof over his head.

"My shift doesn't start until two o'clock tomorrow. I'll visit the community college in the morning to check if Alex could start there in January. Otherwise, he would have to wait until next autumn to continue his studies," she said with the familiar determination in her voice.

"That would be great," Liam said with some hesitation.

"Darling, you are both still young. You can move in together when both of you have a degree," she said.

Liam had to admit that she was right. Still, he was so used to living with Alex that it felt wrong for them to be hundreds of miles apart from each other. *What if Alex doesn't want to wait for years until I graduate?* Liam thought.

They talked for another fifteen minutes and agreed that Liam and Alex would drive to Fairmont as soon as their exams were over. Then Liam hung up the call and turned to Alex. He ran his fingers through his hair as he explained what they had just agreed upon, even though Alex had heard most of the conversation.

"Your parents are good people," Alex said, unable to hide his disappointment that he had to move away from Eddington.

"What if I apply to the community college, too?" Liam said.

"No!" Alex said. "Eastwood has the best history program in the country. You quitting college because of me is out of the question."

Alex was right. Liam had loved Eastwood University from the first day he arrived on campus. The professors were cool, and the other students shared his interests. For the first time in his life, he felt that he fit in somewhere. Not having Alex there would be a significant gap, but deep in his heart, Liam knew that he belonged here.

"They should be able to transfer your credits from here to Fairmont Community College," Liam said.

"Yeah," Alex replied like he didn't care.

"Okay, but maybe I should let you study for a while. You have an exam tomorrow," Liam said and took a book from the table.

"I'm not going to take the exam," Alex said.

Liam looked at his boyfriend and couldn't believe what he had just heard. Ignoring Liam's glare, Alex opened his laptop and started to play a game. Liam stood up and pressed the power button on Alex's laptop.

"What the fuck are you doing?" Alex said, angrier than he had intended.

"You have an exam tomorrow," Liam said.

"Like I said, I'm not taking it," Alex said and turned to look at Liam. "What part of that can't you understand?" he added, knowing that it would piss off his boyfriend.

"You're an asshole. I buy you food, and I get you a place to live, and this is how you thank me?" Liam yelled.

"Yes, Mister Perfect, this is exactly how I thank you," Alex said and rushed out of the room, slamming the door behind him.

Breathing heavily, Alex marched out of the building and stopped only when he felt the cold wind against his face. He had left his keys and phone in the room, and he had no intention of going back to get them, even if Liam would open the door for him. Alex was shaking, but not because of the cold weather.

I'm not like my father, he thought, frightened as he realized that he had almost hit Liam with his fist. Luckily, he had chosen the other alternative he was good at: escaping from his difficulties.

Without a destination, Alex walked away from campus. He was angry at Liam, who couldn't understand his situation, but even angrier at himself. He couldn't return to their room before he had calmed down, but at the same time, the pullover didn't protect him from the cold and windy weather.

Alex saw the gay bar and darted across the street on impulse. Nobody asked for his ID when he stepped in. The place was gloomy and filled with loud music. The few customers glanced at Alex, who was about to turn and leave.

"Hello, handsome. Come here and drink with me," a young man sitting near the window shouted as he held up the shot glass in his hand.

Whatever, Alex thought. He took the glass from the man's hand and downed it with one gulp. It burned his throat, but Alex didn't care.

"Please, sit down, and I'll get us more," the man said with a smile before he left for the bar counter.

Soon, the man came back carrying a tray with ten shot glasses. Alex scanned him and assumed that he was a bit older than Alex. His drinking buddy was dressed in jeans and a jacket, and he was quite cute. His hair, watch and leather shoes indicated that he was wealthy, too.

Perfect, at least he won't make me pay for these, Alex thought and took the glass that the man was offering him.

"By the way, I'm Xavier," the man said and offered his hand.

"Um, Alex," Alex said and shook his hand.

"Nice to meet you, Alex," Xavier said as he put his shot glass on the table.

Alex drank two more glasses that Xavier was generously offering him. Soon, he began to relax enough to look around. Alex saw two boys kissing each other on the other side of the bar. They were around his age and served as a painful reminder of Liam. Alex turned his face back to Xavier, who was smiling at him in a friendly way.

"You study here at Eastwood?" Xavier asked.

"Yes, I'm a freshman," Alex said.

"I graduated two years ago. Business Administration," Xavier said. "I own a small business now with a couple of my friends."

"Cool," Alex said, not knowing what else he should say.

Xavier told Alex about his interior design business. They had a small shop in Eddington, which also provided photography services, but the majority of their sales took place on the internet. Alex was impressed with how easy it sounded.

"You said you study software engineering," Xavier said. "Would you be interested in helping us now and then?"

"Sure," Alex said, even though he knew he would be in Eddington only a couple of days.

"Great," Xavier said and gave Alex a new shot glass. "I'll pay you for your services, one way or another," he added with a smirk.

I can think of many ways, Alex thought and didn't realize that he was quite drunk already. Maybe Xavier would offer him a place to live, too. Then Alex wouldn't be at the mercy of his boyfriend's charity, and he wouldn't have to move back to Fairmont, which he hated from the bottom of his heart.

"Would you mind continuing the night at my place?" Xavier asked as if he were reading Alex's mind.

"Sure," Alex said as he tried to stand up. Unfortunately, he was too drunk and would have fallen without Xavier helping him.

"Wait. I'll walk you there. My house isn't far from here," Xavier said and took a better hold of Alex.

The bartender laughed at them and kept the door open as Xavier helped Alex out of the bar. The other customers didn't pay them any attention when they disappeared into the darkness of the night.

Chapter 17

After swim practice, Tyler and Elyo walked to the pizzeria near campus. Dissatisfied with their performance, the coach had made them sweat, and now both of them were starving.

"Okay if we share the pizza? It's quite late already," Tyler said and opened the door for Elyo.

"I'm so hungry I could eat a horse," Elyo said.

"That's quite a lot for such a small guy," Tyler said.

"Ha-ha," Elyo said. "Okay, let's share. They're huge anyway."

There were no other customers at this time of the night, and the swimmers decided to sit by the window. Their order came ten minutes later, and Elyo already regretted his decision not to order a whole pizza.

"Do you know if Alex is sick or something?" Elyo asked. "He wasn't in class or at the swim club meeting today."

"No idea. Maybe he's studying for the signal processing exam. It's tomorrow," Tyler said and cut the pizza into two halves.

"I'm jealous of him. You know, he lives with his boyfriend," Elyo said. "He gets laid whenever he wants."

"What? Your roommate doesn't help you?" Tyler asked and acted surprised.

Elyo laughed. "Sorry, mate. I play on a different team," he said. "Not that I have any problems with the other team's members."

They kept eating, and Tyler began to joke about them being on a date and sharing their pizza. The small Filipino smiled at him. Tyler was a fun guy to hang around with, and Elyo wasn't the only one who thought so. Everybody on the swim team liked the easygoing jock.

"Since we're on a date, I expect you to pay," Elyo said when the waitress brought the check.

"Wait," Tyler said and looked out of the window.

"I was just kidding."

"I know, but isn't that Alex?"

Now both of them had their faces to the window, and they tried to recognize the guy who entered the gay bar on the other side of the street. It was dark, but the street light was illuminating the area in front of the bar.

"It's him. I would recognize that ass anywhere," Tyler said.

"Dude, that's gross," Elyo said but couldn't help laughing.

"I'm just surprised because I didn't see Liam," Tyler said.

"Maybe he was there already."

Tyler nodded. Besides, it was none of his business where Alex spent the night. Shifting his focus back to the bill, Tyler took his wallet out and began to count his dollars. Elyo had already added enough money to cover his part of the bill.

Tyler and Elyo left the pizzeria and crossed the street. When they came to the place where the gay bar was, they slowed their walking and Tyler tried to see in through the window. Unfortunately, it was too dark, and he couldn't see anything.

"Wanna go in?" Elyo asked.

"Are you asking me on a date or something?" Tyler said.

"Douchebag," Elyo said, and they began walking toward campus.

Glad that he would go home the following day, Shawn rolled his chair along the hospital corridor. The nurse would have brought his supper to the room, but he had wanted to eat in the cafeteria. He had spent enough time in the room already.

Without trouble, the thin high school senior levered himself from the wheelchair back to the bed. His right leg was working normally, but the other leg was still too weak for walking. Shawn would have wanted to use crutches, but the doctor said that it would be too risky because of the movement disorder in his right arm.

The hospital was able to schedule him an hour of physical therapy per day. It had helped his leg to become stronger, but Shawn would have liked to practice walking more. He didn't want to sit in the chair when he returned to school in January.

Maybe someone could help me exercise at home, Shawn thought and realized that it wouldn't be Jamal. His first boyfriend had broken up with him because the media had been so interested in Shawn, and Jamal was worried that his grandmother would find out about their relationship. Ironically, the media had dropped their interest as soon as they realized that Shawn wouldn't die.

Losing Jamal had hurt Shawn more than he was ready to admit. There had been something in the kind and quiet boy that appealed to him. They hadn't even had sex yet, which was surprising considering that they were two horny high school boys. Kissing, they had done a lot, and Shawn missed the touch of Jamal's soft lips against his.

Fucking coward. I'll find a better one, Shawn thought, displeased that he didn't have his laptop. He decided to visit the dating site as soon as he got home.

Speaking of a coward, Shawn hadn't told Scott yet that he was gay. Actually, he had lied to his big brother and said that he had a girlfriend. They called each other now and then, but Shawn found it too difficult to say it on the phone. So, he decided to write his brother an email tomorrow.

Shawn Abrahamson had a plan now. One more night in the hospital bed, and then he would be home.

Scott was studying in their room when Tyler arrived from the pizzeria. Both of them had an exam the following day, Scott in math and Tyler in signal processing. As Tyler's exam wasn't until the evening, he had decided not to study tonight. Besides, it was getting late, and he felt tired.

"Have you heard anything about your brother?" Tyler asked.

"He's going home tomorrow," Scott said.

"Cool. Will he be okay?"

"It will take time, but the doctors expect him to be able to walk again."

"How about the arm?"

Scott sighed and told Tyler that the doctors were not optimistic that the movement disorder in Shawn's arm would disappear completely. The more stressed his brother was, the more difficult it was for him to control the arm.

"Shit. That's sad," Tyler said and paused for a moment to think how life was sometimes so unfair. "Do you mind if I watch TV?" he asked then.

"That's fine. I'm too tired to study anyways," Scott said.

Tyler turned on the TV, and they both sat on his bed and watched some candid camera show that they found quite hilarious. When it ended twenty minutes later, they decided to go to sleep. They undressed to their boxers, and Scott switched off the lights.

"Oh, hey," Scott said in the darkness, "have you seen Alex lately?"

"Why are you asking?" Tyler said.

"Liam called me an hour ago, and he was sick with worry because he didn't know where Alex was. They had an argument. He didn't go into the details, but it sounded pretty bad."

Tyler thought for a second, and then he remembered Alex going to the gay bar near the pizzeria. "Get dressed," he said and switched the lights back on.

Three minutes later, Scott and Tyler were running across campus toward the north gate. It was cold and dark, and it had started to drizzle. Soon, they arrived at the bar and noticed that it was still open.

"Are we going to a gay bar?" Scott asked.

"Yes, Texas. It's my first time, too," Tyler said, opened the door and stepped in.

Tyler saw two boys who shared some classes with him kissing at the back of the bar. Otherwise, the room was empty except the bartender who was standing behind the counter and preparing to close the bar.

"What would you like? We're closing soon," he said.

"Actually, I need some information," Tyler said.

"Wow, is this some crime scene investigation, officer?" the bartender joked.

"Something like that," Tyler said and asked the man if he knew anything about Alex.

The bartender looked at Tyler and Scott for a while with a suspicious look on his face. Tyler was sure that the man wouldn't tell them anything useful when he finally opened his mouth.

"You seem genuinely concerned about your friend?" the bartender asked.

"Yes, we are," Tyler said, trying to speed up the conversation.

"A student who fits your description left about five minutes ago with one of the regulars," the bartender said. "God, he was drunk," he added with a laugh.

"Do you have any idea where they were going?" Tyler asked.

"Like you don't know," the bartender said and gestured wanking with his hand.

Tyler was frustrated. This discussion wasn't leading anywhere, and if Alex was drunk and had left with an unknown man, he could be in danger. Tyler decided to try one more time.

"Can you give us the address?" Tyler said. "Please."

"I'm not a fucking investigation agency," the bartender said. "They went out of the door and turned left."

"Let's go," Tyler said to Scott, and they rushed out of the bar and began running along the street as fast as they could. Unfortunately, they had no idea where they should look for their friend.

Chapter 18

Alex was too drunk to stand on his own legs, and Xavier had to walk him. His mother had died, he had lost his father, and now even Liam had tried to send him away. Alex was happy that he had found a friend who could understand him. Maybe he should have visited the gay bar earlier.

I didn't even have to tell him about my problems, and he still understands me, Alex thought and didn't realize how irrational it sounded.

It was raining harder when they turned into a small alley, and Xavier began to search for his keys in his pockets. Alex assumed that they would soon be at their destination, and he inhaled the fresh air to cheer up.

"You live here?" Alex slurred and looked at the beautiful buildings on both sides of the alley.

"Yes," Xavier smiled. "Just wait until you see the apartment on the inside."

"Where's my boyfriend?" Alex asked suddenly.

"You have a boyfriend?" Xavier said and looked disappointed.

Alex kept asking where Liam was, and for a moment, Xavier didn't seem to know what he should do. Then he proposed that they go into his apartment to take a shower and change into dry clothes. He tried to push Alex forward.

"No, I need to find Liam," Alex said.

"Let's search for him in the morning," Xavier suggested. "I can't leave you here in the rain."

Xavier took a better hold of Alex, who was too drunk to object, and soon they were at the front door. Xavier had just put the key in the lock when Alex heard someone calling his name.

"Tyler? Is that you. I'm here!" Alex shouted.

Scott and Tyler appeared in the alley, panting, and saw Alex and Xavier in front of a door, which Xavier had just opened. For a short time, they just stared at each other.

"He's coming with us," Tyler said to Xavier.

"Sure, no problem, guys," Xavier said.

Keeping his eyes on the two big jocks who had appeared in the alley, Xavier moved slowly inside the building and shut the door, making sure that it was locked. He had no intention of fighting with the guys who seemed to be on a mission to rescue their friend and considered him to be an enemy.

"Alex, what's going on?" Tyler asked and took hold of his friend before he fell down.

Staring at nothing with his glassy eyes, Alex tried to explain everything that had happened to him since his mother had died, but Tyler and Scott could understand little of what he slurred. Apparently, the more drunk Alex was, the more talkative he became, but the less he was able to communicate.

"Let's take him to his room," Tyler said to Scott.

"Is Xavier coming?" Alex asked.

"Who?" Scott said before realizing whom Alex was talking about.

"No, not this time," Tyler said with determination in his voice.

It didn't take long for the jocks to get Alex back to the dorm. As their drunken buddy didn't have his key with him, they had to call Liam and wake him up to get inside the building. Tyler saw the expression on Liam's face when he came downstairs to open the front door in his boxers and wasn't sure whether Liam was more relieved or annoyed to see his boyfriend.

They undressed Alex's wet clothes and put him in his bed. He looked at Liam with sadness in his eyes. Then he fell asleep.

"Um, I think we should go," Tyler said.

"Wait. Thanks for bringing him here," Liam said.

"No problem. Anytime," Tyler said.

Liam picked up his t-shirt from the chair next to his bed. After he pulled it on, the three of them left Alex sleeping in the room and went to the hall. It was past midnight, and no one else was around. They sat on the sofas in the corner.

"Where did you find him?" Liam asked, afraid of the answer.

Tyler looked at Scott before he answered, "He went to a bar near the pizzeria. The gay bar. He was drunk, and some older guy was taking Alex to his apartment when we found him."

With tears stinging his eyes, Liam turned his face toward the windows. He recognized that Alex had had a hard time lately, and maybe he couldn't fully understand what his boyfriend was going through. Still, Liam couldn't approve of how Alex tried to solve all his problems. *He's like his dad*, he realized.

"Do you mind if I ask what's going on?" Tyler said.

Liam sighed. "Alex doesn't have money to continue his studies here. He's been expelled," he said.

"Shit," Tyler said, and for the first time in a long time, he felt speechless.

"He's moving to Fairmont and going to the community college there," Liam said.

"I'm so sorry," Tyler said and looked at Liam empathically.

A couple of teardrops rolled down Liam's cheek, but he wasn't sure whether they were because Alex was moving away from him or because their relationship seemed to be approaching its end.

Alex woke up to someone banging on the door. After figuring out that Liam wasn't there, he stood up from the bed to open the door, not realizing that he was naked. It was Tyler who rushed into the room as soon as Alex got the door open.

"Um, you might want to get dressed before we start," Tyler said.

"Start what?" Alex asked and put his hands in front of his morning wood.

Tyler opened the wardrobe and gave Alex clean boxers and a t-shirt. Then he turned around and let Alex put the clothes on. He even made some coffee while Alex went to the bathroom.

"Okay, big boy. Let's study," Tyler said and handed Alex a cup of fresh coffee.

Alex blushed. "Wait, what are we studying?" he said, confused.

"We have a signal processing exam this evening, and I'm going to help you pass it," Tyler said.

"But, I don't—" Alex began to say.

"No buts," Tyler said. "And I know that you're changing to another college," he added.

One more time, Alex tried to protest, but Tyler didn't back off. They sat on Alex's bed, and topic by topic, Tyler explained everything that Alex hadn't understood in class.

At one o'clock, Tyler announced a lunch break. Alex felt uncomfortable and proposed that they eat something that Liam had put in the fridge. Tyler declined the offer and asked Alex to put on his jacket.

"Let's go to the Chinese buffet around the corner," Tyler said. "I'll pay."

"Um, thanks," Alex said.

Apparently, Liam had told Tyler everything. He was grateful that his friend wanted to help him but felt uneasy that he couldn't do anything to compensate Tyler for his help. Anyhow, he followed Tyler to the restaurant.

"Can I be honest with you?" Tyler asked once they had filled their plates and were sitting at a table.

"I guess I don't have a choice," Alex said and gave his friend a shy smile.

"Liam is the kindest person I know," Tyler said and looked Alex directly in the eyes. "I can't understand what you were thinking yesterday when you left the bar with that man."

The smile on Alex's face vanished, and he blushed with embarrassment. He had difficulties in maintaining eye contact with his friend. He had been mad at Liam and wasted as well, but those were hardly legitimate reasons for his behavior.

"I'm sorry. I guess I wasn't thinking anything," Alex said quietly.

"It's not me you should apologize to," Tyler said.

Alex nodded and knew exactly what Tyler meant by that. He had screwed up again, and his only wishes were that Liam would forgive him and that their relationship would hold up even though they would be studying at different colleges.

"And don't get me wrong," Tyler said, "I like you, Alex. You and Liam are two of my best friends here."

"Everything you said is true. And I hope we can be friends even after, you know, I'm no longer studying here," Alex said.

"Of course," Tyler said. "And look … in high school, I dated this girl. She liked me a lot, and I was a total jerk. So, I'm far from perfect myself."

Alex looked at his handsome friend. It wasn't hard to imagine that a high school girl could have a crush on Tyler. Alex had to admit that once, when Liam had left for a lecture early in the morning, he had laid on the bed and jerked off thinking of Tyler naked in the swimming hall shower room. Obviously, he hadn't revealed that to Liam or Tyler.

After lunch, they began studying again. Surprisingly, Liam hadn't returned from his exam, even though it had ended several hours ago. *Maybe he needs time to think*, Alex thought. Tyler had told him that he and Scott had talked with Liam after they had brought Alex to his bed.

By the time Alex and Tyler left for their exam at half past four, Liam hadn't appeared. Alex forced himself to focus on the exam, but as soon as he had finished it, he wanted to find his boyfriend. They had to talk, again.

For the fifth time over the past hour, Liam checked the time on his phone. It was ten past five, and it was safe to assume that Alex and Tyler had already left. Liam picked his books up from the table and walked out of the library.

He hadn't wanted to meet Alex before the exam that Alex had to take, not with the message that he had to tell his boyfriend. It would have ruined all the work that Tyler had done to help Alex with his studies.

Most of the short trip from the library to the dorm, tears were rolling down Liam's cheeks. Luckily, they were mixed with the raindrops, and the other students walking across campus didn't pay any attention to him.

The argument they had had the previous day was just one of many they had had since Alex's mother had died. In addition, his boyfriend had spent a night in jail and soon after gotten into a car accident. And now Alex had been expelled from college. All that, and much more, Liam would have happily accepted, but there was one thing he couldn't handle.

Why isn't he talking to me? Why does he always try to solve all his problems by himself? Liam wondered, remembering again the time when Alex had tried to kill himself less than a year ago.

And why do I still love him so much? Liam thought and blew his nose. He was tired of crying but didn't know how to make it stop.

As soon as Liam got to their room, he pulled their beds apart. He couldn't help himself as he made Alex's bed and set his clothes nicely on the bedcovers. Then he went to the grocery store to make sure that Alex had enough food until they would leave for Fairmont.

Liam had been waiting for an hour, trying to focus on a textbook, when Alex returned from his exam. Liam closed the book and looked at Alex, who had the most remorseful expression on his face. Alex stood at the door and seemed like he was scared to walk farther.

"I'm so sorry," Alex said, and tears welled up in his eyes. Then he saw their beds separated, and his face went pale.

"We need to talk," Liam said calmly, worried that Alex would storm out of the room.

Alex didn't go anywhere, but he sat down on his own bed. "You want to break up," he said, looking at his shoes.

"I want to put us on hold," Liam said. "I love you, but I need time to think. And maybe you need it, too."

Alex sighed. He had wished for another outcome to this discussion, but he had somehow known to prepare for this conclusion. He had screwed up, again. College was supposed to boost their relationship to another level, but now it seemed that it would only separate them.

"Can I still live at your parents' house?" Alex asked.

"Yes, you can," Liam said. It was hard to describe how much he would have wanted to hug Alex, one last time, but he didn't trust himself where it might lead.

They wished each other good night, and then Liam switched off the lights. Two hours later, Liam could still hear how his roommate was rolling on the bed, trying to get sleep.

Chapter 19

A blissful happiness filled Shawn when he rolled his chair to his room. He was home again, for the first time in many weeks. He stood up from the wheelchair and, taking hold of his table, moved slowly toward the office chair. His walking was still unstable, but getting better and better.

Shawn took his laptop and connected the power adapter as the battery was empty. Feeling nervous and impatient, he waited until the computer booted up and he was able to open the email application. It was time to write to Scott.

Hi Brother,

I just got home from the hospital, and it's great to be here again. Like I told you on the phone, the doctors expect my leg to work normally if I just remember to practice it enough. That's the good news. :)

My arm is a bit better but will never work perfectly. When I go back to school, I'll meet a student counselor experienced in people with disabilities who can help me to choose a suitable undergraduate program. Maybe I'll enroll in Eastwood next year.

There's one more thing. The newspapers have written a lot about me. You might have already read the news about the attack being a hate crime, and I can't hide it anymore. Scott, I'm gay. I hope you're not disappointed. It's something that I haven't chosen and can't change. Please, don't be mad.

Love you,
Shawn

It took half an hour for Shawn to rewrite the email over and over again before he was happy with it. Feeling how his heart began to beat faster, he moved the mouse cursor over the send button. Finally, Shawn pressed the button, knowing that there wasn't a way to take it back. He had come out to his brother.

Two hours had passed, and Scott hadn't replied to his email. Shawn began to worry that his brother hadn't taken the news well. Fortunately, Scott would be coming home for Christmas, and Shawn would get a chance to explain. Maybe over time, the big football player would learn to accept it.

Shawn heard a bell ringing and first thought that it was an incoming email from Scott. Then he realized that it was the doorbell. Someone walked to answer the door, and soon his mother called him. It took a while for Shawn to get back to his wheelchair, and when he finally reached the hall, he saw Jamal there.

"Hi," Jamal said and looked at him timidly.

Shawn nodded and wasn't sure what to think about his ex-boyfriend. "What do you want?" he asked, sounding exactly as rude as he had intended.

"Um, I just ... I wanted to see you," Jamal said, taken aback by Shawn's question.

"So, here I am. Take a good look," Shawn said.

Jamal seemed to be more nervous than Shawn had ever seen him, and for a short moment, Shawn almost pitied him. It took some time for Jamal to collect himself and gather his thoughts.

"I'm sorry, Shawn. I was scared, and I was wrong," Jamal said. "Can you forgive me?"

Shawn was about to say something when his right arm twitched and hit on the metal frame of the wheelchair. It was less painful than it was humiliating, especially because Shawn couldn't stop the movement immediately.

"Leave me alone," he snarled at Jamal, who looked sad but began to open the door to leave.

"Okay. Bye then," Jamal said softly and closed the door behind him.

Shawn rolled back to his room, giving his mother a look that communicated clearly that he didn't want to talk about it right now. She would have, anyway, advised him to agree with Jamal, and Shawn wasn't ready to admit that his mother was probably right.

I need to come to terms with Scott first before I can think of dating, Shawn thought and decided to postpone his decision to return to the dating site on the internet. Instead, he checked his email again and found Scott's short reply.

Shawn,

I'm glad to hear that you got home and your leg is getting better. Let's hope the arm gets better over time, too.

About you being gay – I'm not disappointed or mad. I still love you, and I hope you find a cute boyfriend. :)

Looking forward to seeing you soon,
Scott

As happy as Shawn had been to get home from the hospital, he couldn't find the words to describe how happy and relieved he was after reading Scott's email. It turned out that his brother wasn't just a dumb jock after all.

The only thing that shaded Shawn's happiness was that he had just sent Jamal away. Maybe it wasn't too late to fix that mistake.

Chapter 20

It was Christmas Eve, and Fairmont was covered by a thick layer of white snow. Liam was playing the piano, which his father had moved to the living room to make room for the queen-sized bed in Liam's room. Alex sat on the sofa and listened to Liam's angelic voice as he sang "White Christmas."

Liam hadn't told his parents that they had put their relationship on hold. He was sure that his mother could sense the change in their behavior, but she would likely assume it was because Alex would not be returning to Eastwood. Sleeping in the same bed wasn't too uncomfortable, and Alex had honored his wish to keep his hands on his own side.

"That was beautiful," Alex said when Liam had finished the song.

"Thanks," Liam said and smiled at Alex.

"I'll just go see if your mother needs help," Alex said.

Liam stood up from the piano chair, and they were now both standing in the living room looking at each other. There was hardly five feet between them, and Liam felt a pull toward Alex. He just couldn't help it.

Their shoulders touched slightly, which wasn't an accident, when Alex walked to the kitchen where he found Liam's parents setting the table. Mrs. Green thanked Alex for the offer but declined it politely. In her thinking, the boys were their guests of honor. Besides, she wanted to make sure that everything was done the way she had planned. She liked Christmas as much as her son.

"It looks like dinner will be ready soon," Alex said when he returned to the living room.

"Perfect. I'm starving," Liam said.

"Thanks for letting me spend Christmas here. Otherwise, I wouldn't have anywhere to go," Alex said sincerely.

Liam swallowed and, for a brief moment, wanted to hug Alex. It still hurt him that Alex almost cheated on him with some stranger he had met at the bar. On the other hand, after the night when Liam had pulled their beds apart, Alex had focused on his studies and passed all his courses, even signal processing.

Maybe it's a good sign that he's taking responsibility for his future, Liam thought. His mother had arranged things so that Alex could start at Fairmont Community College in January.

"Alex, even though we aren't dating right now, you're still important to me," Liam said, keeping his voice down so that his parents wouldn't hear their discussion.

Alex held back his tears. "You, too," he said, his voice cracking.

"Boys, dinner is ready!" Liam's mother shouted from the kitchen.

"Let's go," Liam said.

Even though he had seen it every year, Liam was still impressed. The kitchen lights were switched off, and there were candles on the table. His father had brought their best tableware from storage, and the table was filled with steaming dishes containing all those delicacies that Liam had been dreaming of ever since they had started the road trip to Fairmont.

"Help yourselves," Liam's mother said, satisfied with the setting.

"Thanks," the boys said at the same time and sat down.

The turkey with cranberry sauce and mashed potatoes were heavenly. All of them ate with good appetites, and there was very little discussion before their plates were empty. Mrs. Green encouraged the boys to take more, and she didn't have to ask twice.

"I'm so happy that you boys found each other," Liam's mother said. "Alex, I can see that you make my son happy."

Alex looked at Liam, feeling uncomfortable that he had to lie to her, but Liam smiled at him and took hold of his hand. Alex wasn't sure if it was just an act but decided to play along.

"Liam is the kindest person I know," Alex said, repeating Tyler's wise words, "and I'm grateful that you let me live here. I'll get a job so that I can pay you," he added.

"Absolutely not," Mrs. Green said. "You're a part of the family, and we want you to focus on your studies."

"Um, but isn't me living here for free a bit too much?" Alex hesitated. "At least, I want to help with cleaning and other household work."

"We are happy to have you here, Alex," Mrs. Green said, "and we want you to graduate with good grades. If you can promise that, then I'll let you help."

"Thanks, Mrs. Green. I promise," Alex said and felt Liam squeezing his hand.

"Oh God, please stop calling me 'Mrs. Green,'" Liam's mother said, smiling. "It makes me feel so old."

"Yes, ma'am," Alex said, and she rolled her eyes.

They spent a nice evening together talking, eating and playing cards. Half an hour after midnight, they were all so tired that they decided to go to bed. Alex and Liam went to their bedroom and closed the door.

"I have a small gift for you," Alex said and gave Liam a shy smile.

Liam looked at him, surprised. "But we agreed not to buy anything," he said, knowing how little money Alex had.

"I know that I have screwed up badly," Alex said and swallowed. "You'll be going back to Eddington soon, and I wanted you to have at least one good memory of me."

Liam couldn't hold back tears. "I do have plenty of good memories of you," he said, and his voice cracked.

Alex took a small photo frame from his bag. Inside the frame, there was a picture of them that their friend, Tristan, had taken on their high school prom night. Alex gave it to Liam, who held it in his hands like it was his most precious thing.

Tears were rolling from their eyes, and neither of them was able to say anything. Then Liam moved closer and hugged Alex briefly. It may have looked like a friendly hug, but it meant much more to both of them.

"Thanks. I'll keep this on my table," Liam said when he was finally able to speak. Alex smiled at him.

Then they undressed and crawled under the blanket. They wished each other good night and began sleeping. Nothing more happened, and it felt like it was meant to be like that.

The day after Christmas, Alex knocked on the door of his father's apartment. He had chosen to come here in the morning, not too early that he would be still sleeping but early enough to make sure that his father was still sober. At least, he hoped so.

"What do you want?" Mr. Wesley said after seeing his son standing on the porch.

"To talk to you," Alex said and stepped in.

The apartment was a mess. Nobody had washed the dishes for weeks, and the small table in front of the sofa was full of empty beer bottles. Alex wasn't surprised how his father was spending the money he had got after selling their big house.

I don't want to end up living like this. I'm not like him, Alex thought but forced a neutral expression on his face. He hadn't come here to judge his father.

"Dad, I want to talk to you," Alex said.

"You're not my son, faggot," Mr. Wesley replied, and Alex realized that he looked ten years older than when they had met the previous time.

"I'm your son, whether you like it or not. And since Mom is dead, it's just you and me," Alex said, ignoring his father's attempt to insult him.

His father snorted. He had no idea where this discussion was going, but he decided to listen, assuming that was the quickest way to get rid of his unwanted guest.

"I can see that my being gay is troubling you, and maybe it's best that we don't see each other for some time," Alex said.

"You got that right," his father said.

"But whenever you're ready, let me know. I don't want us to part on bad terms," Alex said and walked out of the door.

He expected his father to yell something after him, call him names or wish him a safe trip to Hell, but he couldn't hear anything. Once he was on the sidewalk, Alex turned to look back and saw how his father first glared at him and then slammed the door.

The ball is in your court, old man, Alex thought and walked to his car. In fact, he felt proud of the way he had handled the situation. Maybe he wouldn't ever see his father again, but he had done his part.

"How did it go?" Liam asked as soon as he had slid into the car.

"Actually, quite well," Alex said, and smiled to himself.

"He's okay with you being gay?" Liam said, surprised.

"No, but I'm okay with him being not okay," Alex replied mysteriously.

The trip back to Liam's house reminded Alex of their time at Fairmont High School. He had given Liam a ride home many times, and the only difference was that this time, they were not holding hands while Alex was driving. Alex hoped that someday that would change.

Far too soon, it was the last morning of Liam's Christmas break. Alex watched with a sad expression on his face as Liam packed his clothes in the suitcase. Both of them knew that it could be months before they saw each other again.

"I can drive you to Eddington," Alex said, trying to avoid the inevitable.

"Thanks, but you would have to drive six hours there and another six hours back," Liam said. "Besides, it would be too painful to sit in the car that long, knowing that you won't be staying."

Alex felt a spark of relief. Liam indeed had feelings for him. Alex checked that Liam's parents weren't anywhere near, and then he closed the bedroom door. He cleared his throat to gather courage.

"Can I hug you?" Alex asked, and every cell in his body was afraid that Liam would say no.

"Sure," Liam said and flashed Alex a broad smile.

They wrapped their arms around each other. Their eyes were moist, and neither of them wanted to let go. Alex felt Liam's warm body against his, and no matter how tightly he held Liam, he felt that he couldn't get close enough to him. Then Liam kissed him.

"I love you," Liam whispered in Alex's ear.

Alex couldn't hold back his tears anymore. "I love you, too," he said, but his voice cracked so badly that nobody else but Liam could have understood his words.

Liam locked the door, and in a few seconds, they had ripped off their clothes and were lying on the bed, wrapped in each other. Alex couldn't remember the last time he had been as aroused as that moment. He didn't last long, but it was the best sex ever.

"Does this mean that we're a couple again?" Alex asked, and this time, he was pretty sure he knew the answer.

"If it's okay with you," Liam said and kissed Alex.

"Definitely," Alex said, smiling at his cute boyfriend.

After Liam had packed his things, they decided to go for a walk. They still had a couple of hours before Liam's bus would leave the Fairmont bus terminal, and the weather was sunny even though it was cold.

"My program will take two years, and then I can move to Eddington," Alex said. "Maybe we could move in together and live there until you graduate," he added.

"I would love that," Liam said, "and, of course, I'll come here in summer and for Christmas break."

Alex tried to stay positive, but it was hard. "I'm going to miss you," he said finally.

"Me too," Liam said.

They hugged, ignoring the other people who might see them. Alex felt happy that he had gotten Liam back. They could email or talk on the phone to each other every day, which they quite likely would do, but this was one of his last chances for months to touch Liam and feel his boyfriend's body close to him.

And then, all too soon, Liam was sitting on the bus, alone, traveling to Eddington.

Chapter 21

The bus left Liam near the Eastwood University campus, and he approached the dorm with mixed feelings. It was nice to regroup with all his friends, but the most important person was missing. Alex wasn't there. Feeling empty, Liam opened the front door, walked up the stairs and approached his room.

I wonder what kind of roommate they have assigned me, Liam thought as he put the key in the lock. He was surprised to find the room empty. His new roommate hadn't arrived yet.

It was Monday evening, and courses wouldn't start until Wednesday. Liam was concerned that his new roommate would be some laid-back party boy, who left all his school activities to the very last moment. Alex had always given him peace to study.

Liam decided to call Alex and let him know that he had arrived on campus safely. Hearing his voice would be bittersweet, but Liam missed his boyfriend already. Actually, he had spent half of the bus ride crying like a baby. It was strange that nobody had come to ask if he was okay.

Why isn't he answering? Liam thought when he tried to call Alex for the third time. Worried that something had happened, he was about to call his parents but decided not to. Maybe Alex needed time to adjust to this new situation. It wasn't easy to move from one of the best universities in the country to a community college, and Liam was sad that he couldn't do more to help Alex.

What if we grow apart? he asked himself and realized that he had to stop thinking the worst or he would go nuts before classes even started.

Tired from traveling, Liam decided to take a shower before he went to bed. The shower room was empty, and Liam spent at least half an hour under the hot water analyzing their situation. The conclusion was always the same; he wouldn't see Alex before spring break.

Feeling lonelier than he had in a long time, Liam walked through the quiet building back to his room. When he was about to open the door, he heard some noise and assumed that his roommate had finally arrived.

God damn, I'm practically naked, Liam thought and made sure that the towel was wrapped tightly around his waist. Then he entered the room, only to find that it was empty. Maybe the noise had come from some other place.

Liam checked his phone one last time, and there were still no calls or messages from Alex. Feeling a bit annoyed at his boyfriend for not responding to his calls, he switched off the lights and went to bed.

As he had guessed, he spent most of the night thinking of Alex.

The following morning, after a couple of hours of sleep, Liam stood up from his bed. He wasn't sure which one was worse, his headache or the fact that there still weren't any messages or calls from Alex.

He was already searching for Alex's number from his favorites list when he decided that it was better to let his boyfriend call him when he was ready. Liam was sure that Alex hadn't forgotten him yet. The memory of them having sex on their last day together in Fairmont was still fresh in Liam's mind, and it made him smile.

After taking some medicine for the headache, Liam left for breakfast. As his fridge was empty, he opted to eat in the student canteen, which should be open already even though classes weren't starting until the following day.

There were plenty of students walking in the same direction, and Liam recognized some familiar faces. A guy coming from the canteen looked so much like Alex that Liam had to turn his face to avoid looking at him, but it didn't help. Everywhere he looked, he saw places that reminded him of his boyfriend.

I can do this, Liam thought and stepped into the canteen. He paid for the buffet breakfast at the desk and took a tray. Once he had filled his plate, he spotted Tyler and Scott sitting on the right. Scott raised his hand to invite Liam to their table.

"Hi, nice to see you," Liam said and noticed that two other boys were sitting together with them.

"Hi, Liam. This is my brother Shawn," Scott introduced the thin boy sitting next to him. "And Shawn's boyfriend Jamal," he added, looking at the teen on the other side of the table.

Scott explained that Shawn and Jamal had come to visit him as their winter quarter didn't start until the following Monday. Liam looked at the high school seniors, and couldn't help thinking about Alex, again. To him, Shawn and Jamal seemed a happy couple, and he wished that life was easier for them than it had been for him and Alex. Then he noticed how Shawn's arm made an uncontrollable movement and realized that maybe life wasn't meant to be easy for anyone.

"Shawn got a scholarship from the American Rainbow Association. He starts his studies here next autumn," Scott said, and Liam recognized the pride in his voice.

"Cool, congratulations!" Liam said and smiled at the boy, who was beaming.

"Actually, it was Tyler's idea. He found the application form on the internet," Scott said.

"I'm the good fairy," Tyler said.

"The good fairy of all fairies," Shawn said.

Once they had finished their breakfast, Jamal helped Shawn to stand up, and they walked slowly through the canteen to the exit. Shawn was walking quite well already, even though Jamal and Scott had to help him down the stairs. After the last stair, Shawn thanked his boyfriend for the help by kissing him.

"You're not gonna kiss Scott, too?" Tyler teased him.

"Nah, I leave that to you, man," Shawn said.

"Eww," Scott said. "No offense," he added.

Scott wanted to show Shawn and Jamal the main building and the library, so Liam and Tyler began walking back to the dorms. It was nice to hang around with someone now than Alex wasn't here anymore.

"Do you mind if I stop by later today?" Tyler asked like he had read Liam's thoughts.

"Sure, that would be cool," Liam said.

"By the way, how's Alex?"

"I don't know. I haven't heard anything from him since I left Fairmont."

"Maybe you'll hear from him soon. Who knows?"

Liam entered the dorm and kept thinking about Tyler's last comment. It sounded odd, but maybe Tyler had just wanted to comfort him. He looked back through the glass door, but Tyler was already so far away that Liam decided to let it be.

He opened the door to his room and found the other bed still empty. Whoever his roommate would be, he wasn't in any hurry. It didn't look promising, but Liam could do nothing but wait.

It was three in the afternoon when Liam finally heard someone unlocking the door. He stood up from the bed and checked the mirror to make sure his hair looked good. When he turned around, his jaw dropped.

"What are you doing here?" Liam asked.

"I'm happy to see you, too," Alex said, smiling. "Wanted to surprise you," he added.

"Cool! But doesn't it take six hours for you to drive back?"

"I'm not going back."

Only then did Liam realize that Alex was carrying two suitcases with him. He was even more confused when Alex lifted the other bag on the empty bed and opened it. It was filled with his clothes.

"Something very weird happened to me yesterday," Alex said.

Words failed Liam. He just stood there with his mouth open.

"I got a call from some American Rainbow Association or something," Alex said. "They told me that they had approved my scholarship application, and I can continue my studies here."

A broad smile appeared on Liam's face, and he rushed to hug his boyfriend. This was the best surprise ever, and he had to pinch first Alex and then himself to be sure that this was really happening.

"The funny thing is that I haven't even filled out any scholarship application," Alex said.

"I have an idea who did it," Liam said and smiled mysteriously.

"You?" Alex asked.

"Tyler."

Liam helped Alex to put his clothes into the wardrobe, and then they pushed the beds together and took off their clothes. Alex warned him that he might be a bit sweaty after the long trip. Liam didn't mind but promised that Alex would be even sweatier soon. He was right, of course.

An hour later, they were lying naked on the bed and kissing when someone knocked on the door. Quickly, they dressed before Liam opened the door. It was Tyler.

"Oh, Alex. Nice to see you," Tyler said.

"You don't look too surprised, so I take it you might be the reason I'm here," Alex said.

"I might be," Tyler said, smiling.

"Thanks, man," Alex said and hugged his friend.

Tyler wrapped his long arms around Alex and squeezed him tightly. Tyler was a real friend, and Alex had no idea how he could ever compensate him for all he had done.

"Can we stop this before it becomes too gay?" Tyler said and patted Alex on his butt before letting go of him.

"Thanks, Tyler. What you did is beyond awesome," Liam said.

"I don't understand gay guys," Tyler said and rolled his eyes. "I hug your boyfriend and grope his ass, and all you do is thank me."

Alex laughed. It felt so good to be back in Eddington and see all his friends. And, of course, Liam.

Epilogue

On Saturday morning after the first week of the spring semester, Alex and Liam slept in. They had no plans for the day. Liam woke up a bit earlier than Alex. After watching his sleeping boyfriend for a while, he left the room to take a shower.

Alex heard Liam coming back and closing the door. Feeling drowsy, he raised his head and smiled at Liam, who was getting dressed. Liam blew him a kiss and started the coffee machine. Soon, the aroma of fresh coffee filled the room.

"I'm so happy to be here," Alex said.

Liam looked at Alex with his sparkling eyes. "I'm happy that you are here, too," he said.

"Actually, I'm this happy," Alex smirked and moved the blanket so that Liam could see his erection.

"Wait for me there, big boy," Liam said eagerly as he finished filling his coffee mug.

Liam kissed his boyfriend and sat on his lap, waiting for Alex to wrap his arms around him. Liam loved the position; it made him feel safe and loved. It was like Alex's strong arms were protecting him against any possible threat.

"I love you," Alex murmured in his ear.

"I love you, too," Liam said and felt at ease.

"I'm sorry for … what I did," Alex said. Liam felt how his boyfriend tensed a bit behind him.

"Alex, we talked it through already," Liam said.

Both of them wanted to start a new chapter in their relationship, and it seemed like it was finally possible. Alex's scholarship from the American Rainbow Association covered his tuition fees, and he had taken a small student loan to cover housing, books, and food. Later, he could even find a job, but right now he wanted to focus on getting his studies back on track.

Alex knew that there were still things to do before he could truly feel that he deserved Liam's full trust, but he was more determined than ever to get it back. Actually, he even hoped to someday be engaged to Liam. But that would be another story. Right now, he was happy that they were together again.

Liam's phone began ringing, and he put his coffee mug aside to take the phone from his pocket. It was his mother, who wanted to know how her son was doing now than Alex was back in Eddington. Liam had hardly said the first sentence when Alex opened the fly of his jeans and put his hand inside his boxers.

God damn, I have a good idea where this leads, Liam thought, feeling Alex fondling his rapidly growing erection. He didn't mind, though. He had his boyfriend back, and nothing could feel better than that.

About the Author

Jay Argent is a novelist in his forties who lives a peaceful life with his husband. His favorite hobbies are music, movies, and romantic novels. He obtained a degree in engineering in 2001 and built a successful career in a management consulting firm. Using his own high school and college experiences as inspiration, he is now pursuing his true passion of writing.

If you have any feedback, you can contact him by email at jay@jayargent.com. He very much looks forward to hearing from you.

http://jayargent.com

Printed in Great Britain
by Amazon